Home Fires

ILLINOIS SHORT FICTION

Crossings by Stephen Minot
A Season for Unnatural Causes by Philip F. O'Connor
Curving Road by John Stewart
Such Waltzing Was Not Easy by Gordon Weaver

Rolling All the Time by James Ballard
Love in the Winter by Daniel Curley
To Byzantium by Andrew Fetler
Small Moments by Nancy Huddleston Packer

One More River by Lester Goldberg
The Tennis Player by Kent Nelson
A Horse of Another Color by Carolyn Osborn
The Pleasures of Manhood by Robley Wilson, Jr.

The New World by Russell Banks
The Actes and Monuments by John William Corrington
Virginia Reels by William Hoffman
Up Where I Used to Live by Max Schott

The Return of Service by Jonathan Baumbach
On the Edge of the Desert by Gladys Swan
Surviving Adverse Seasons by Barry Targan
The Gasoline Wars by Jean Thompson

Desirable Aliens by John Bovey
Naming Things by H. E. Francis
Transports and Disgraces by Robert Henson
The Calling by Mary Gray Hughes

Into the Wind by Robert Henderson
Breaking and Entering by Peter Makuck
The Four Corners of the House by Abraham Rothberg
Ladies Who Knit for a Living by Anthony E. Stockanes

Pastorale by Susan Engberg
Home Fires by David Long
The Canyons of Grace by Levi S. Peterson
Babaru by B. Wongar

HOME FIRES

Stories by

David Long

UNIVERSITY OF ILLINOIS PRESS

Urbana Chicago London

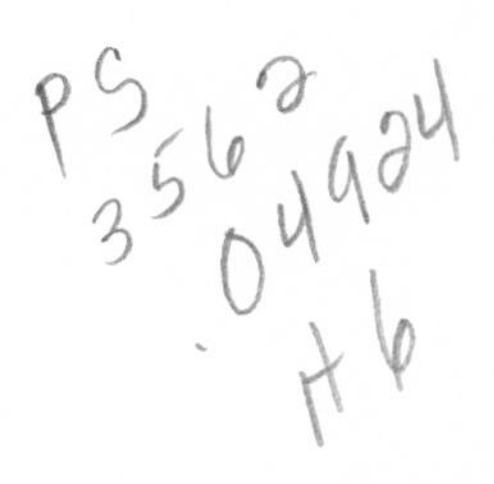

Publication of this work was supported in part
by grants from the National Endowment for the Arts
and the Illinois Arts Council, a state agency.

Manufactured in the United States of America

"Eclipse," *fiction international,* 12 (1980); reprinted in *The Pushcart Prize,* VI (1981–82)
"Life As We Know It," *Intro #6* (Anchor Books, 1974)
"Saving Graces," *The Denver Quarterly*, 15, no. 3 (1981)
"Other People's Stories," forthcoming in *Sewanee Review*
"Like Some Distant Crying," *Carolina Quarterly,* 34, no. 1 (Summer 1981)
"Home Fires," *Canto,* 3, no. 3 (1980)

Library of Congress Cataloging in Publication Data

Long, David, 1948-
Home fires: stories.

(Illinois short fiction)
Contents: Eclipse—Life as we know it—Border crossing—[etc.]
I. Title. II. Series.
PS3562.04924H6 813'.54 82-4927
ISBN 0-252-00991-6 (cloth) AACR2
ISBN 0-252-00992-4 (paper)

For Suzy

Contents

Eclipse

I came home on borrowed rides, east across the sun-blinded distances of Nevada and Utah, north into the forests of Montana, slouched on the cracked seats of pickups, remembering indistinctly what had taken me away and more vividly what I had found. In the back of my mind was the idea that being home would put an end to it. The green-painted man was dead in the bathtub, overdosed beyond bliss. The shower head had dripped all night on his startled face, rivulets of poster paint streaking the porcelain, as if the life inside him had putrified and drained itself. He was nobody I knew. None of them were. So I had stepped into the early morning glare, made my way out of San Pedro's dockyards, squinting at the furious light, fighting off the stink of casualties. The curiosity had burned off me like a dusting of black powder. It was nothing religious after all, only rumors and attractions, an itch in the bloodstream I had taken with full seriousness. The Indian dropped me on the corner by the western-wear store. "Hey, you take care of yourself," he yelled, pulling away, the beer cans rattling in the empty bed of his truck.

The wind blew dust in my eyes. I recognized nobody on the streets. I found that the wave that had carried off so many of us who grew up here had left only the most stubborn, and in my absence they had made families and leaned into their work as if they were born to it. I felt born to no work in particular and had long ago been absolved of kin, having no brothers or sisters, a father who had filled his veins with a substance used to euthanize household pets, and a mother who had found religion in an Arizona retirement community. Though I figured it was as much mine as anyone's, I was not carefully remembered in this town, and I thought I could use this fact to begin a normal, unobtrusive life for myself. Within a year I married Johanna, a big, pleasant girl whose red curls hung thick and guileless around her shoulders, whose skin smelled of salt and flour, who tended to simple jokes and loose clothes of khaki and checked flannel. If she was on a quest it was for nothing ethereal or terribly hard to locate. I must have seemed like a survivor of distant wickedness, a man in need of good intentions. It was true, and I was grateful for the real affection she lavished on me, never understanding it clearly, always fearful she loved the mothering more than its damaged object. I ate her carob cookies, her hardly raised soybean breads, her breakfast rolls suffocating in honey. I never yelled, I never threatened. After suppers on late summer nights, after the thunderstorms had cleared the air, we'd walk the bank of the low-running river, the swifts darting around our heads, the silence between us comfortable enough. I would watch her sit in the debris of washed-up stones, her soft chin lifted to the light as she studied the familiar pattern of mountains that surrounded us, her eyes unable to hide their satisfaction. Saturday nights we drank Lucky Lager at the Amvets and danced around and round to the soothing tunes of Jan Dell and her band, Johanna's favorite. Home again in the insulated darkness of the trailer's bedroom, she would clutch me, so full and earnest I thought I had succumbed—to her, to every bit of it.

Johanna's father, Darrell, was the district Petrolane distributor, and, though he took me with suspicion, he was persuaded to give me a job driving one of his gas trucks. Every day I followed a lazy loop of junctions and wheat towns, contemplating the horizon—stubbled or rich-tasseled, depending on the season. Sometimes the sheer size of the panorama gave me a taste of the planet's curvature, a glimpse of the big picture, but I couldn't hold it. When I stopped, I would stand by the truck and listen to the troubles of the ranchers, nodding as if I truly sympathized. Every night I came home and kicked my boots off and stretched out on the recliner by the TV like a thousand other husbands in town.

Johanna had a son the next year, and when he had grown past earliest infancy he looked so much like her I saw none of myself in him. She named him Eric after her father's father who had died some months before. He was solid and cheerful, everything I was not. Johanna grew less tolerant. When she wanted to lighten my mood, she would come and tell me, "You have a boy you can be proud of." It was not pride but panic I felt. I would often wake and see his round clear-eyed face inches from mine as though he had stood for hours waiting for me. I knew there was something that should flow between us, as unasked for as spring water or moonlight. At night I would lay him in the bottom of the bunkbed he, so far, shared with only the dark room. I would try to make up stories to send him off to a good sleep. Nothing came.

"Tell him what it was like when you were a boy," Johanna said. "He'd like *anything* from you."

"It's a blur," I told her.

"What is it with you?" she said.

"If I knew, I'd fix it," I said.

"Would you?"

I turned away from her and went out and started the pickup and backed it out as far as the mailboxes and couldn't decide which way to turn. I shut off the engine and in a moment lay down on the bench seat and tried to clear my head. I fell asleep hugging myself in the cool November air. When I woke, there was a skim of snow on the hood of the truck. I walked back to the trailer. She had left a message on the refrigerator door, spelled out in Eric's magnetic letters. *Give or Go.* I went to the bedroom. A brittle ballad was coming from the clock radio. "Listen," I said, shaking her shoulder, but she was deep asleep.

One Friday afternoon, after the long, wasting winter had gone, I came home from my route, later than normal since I'd stopped along the way for two Happy Hours, and found Johanna and Eric gone. In fact, it was all gone, the trailer house and everything. I climbed out of the truck, dumb-struck, a fine rain soaking my hair. Deep tracks curled through the shoots of pale grass I'd finally made grow. The muddy plywood skirts were strewn like a busted poker hand. I was wiped clean. The only thing left on the lot was the empty dog house, canted and streaked after a bad season.

In his office the next morning Darrell handed me my last paycheck in a licked-shut envelope and went back to what he was doing, punching digits on his pocket calculator as if they were bugs.

"That all you're going to tell me?" I asked him.

"That's about got it," Darrell said.

"What'd I do? Tell me that?"

Darrell's eyes disappeared in a squinty smile. He slid the snoose around inside his mouth.

"Near as I can tell," Darrell said, "you didn't do a goddamn thing."

I took a third-story room at the Frontier Hotel and sat on the cold radiator and watched the spavined old horse-breakers limp in and out of the cafe across the street, their straw hats stuck to their heads like barnacles. I quietly considered the loss of my wife and child and felt nothing sharp—except surprise, and when I focused on that I realized that the breakup had been a sure thing all along. Her letter came without a return address. Don't worry, she said, she wouldn't be hounding me for money, Darrell had taken care of her. About Eric she said: *He won't remember you. I believe it's just as well.* About her reasons she said only: *I'm sorry; I won't be your rest cure.*

The sun finally took control of the valley. Lilacs flowered outside the dentist's office, road crews patched chuck holes up and down Main Street, the foothills shone in a green mist above the roof of the abandoned Opera House. Strangers nodded *howdy* on the sidewalks. Everything was repairing itself, and I was out of time with it. Years before, I had felt myself choking in this town and blamed its narrow imagination, and had gone off looking for something Bigger Than Life. Now I didn't have the heart to move nor any trace of destination.

I found work at a small outfit south of town that manufactured camper shells for pickups. There I met Clevinger, a scrawny, tiny-eyed man my age, a twice-wounded survivor of Vietnam patrols. He'd worn the others out with his chatter and fixed on me as soon as I arrived. I listened as long as I could. Clevinger's idea of heaven was twenty acres up the North Fork, heavily timbered and remote, a place to disappear to. Every afternoon after work he drove out and looked at parcels of land that only a few years earlier he might have afforded, and every morning he jabbered about the bastards who owned the money. As he talked, he flexed the muscles in his arms, as white and hard as if they had grown underground. He was a man who'd changed, so certainly I didn't need to know how he'd been before. It showed as visibly as cracks running across his face. Seeing him like that made me know that I was not so different, though I had nothing like jungle warfare to blame it on.

It was a hot, rainless summer. The wilderness areas flared with fire time and again, and one afternoon in early September a burn started in a tinder-dry draw near town and crept over the nearby foothills. Clevinger and I left the shop and stood in the parking lot watching the black smoke billow above the fireline. A World War II bomber rumbled over our heads and banked toward the trees, spraying bright reddish streams of fire retardant, through which the sunlight came streaked and bloody. Clevinger said nothing, his arms hugged tight against his skinny chest, the pale skin around his eyes jerking as the smoke drifted over us. It was the next day Clevinger exploded in the shop. All of a sudden he was down in a fiery-eyed crouch, strafing the room with his pneumatic nailing gun. I was caught in the open, carrying a half-built assemblage with a boy named Buster. Clevinger hit us both. The first cleat took Buster above the wrist; he yipped and let go of his end, the weight of it all falling to me. My back snapped like a pop bead. As I went down a second cleat shot through my mouth, taking with it slivers of jawbone.

I lay flat on the concrete, choking on pain, staring up at the moldering light coming through the Quonset's skylight, hearing shouts and grunts and finally the sound of metal striking Clevinger's skull. For weeks afterward I could see the dark luster of Clevinger's eyes, the look that said it didn't matter who we were. It was nothing personal.

My back was badly torn but would heal if I behaved myself. My jaw had to be wired. When they let me out of the hospital, I returned to my room at the Frontier and ate broth and Instant Breakfasts and anything else I could get to seep through my closed teeth. I called

Workman's Comp and discovered I was the victim of a policy called the Coordination of Benefits. My caseworker, Wayne, treated me like I was both childlike and dangerous. It was months before I saw a dollar. In the meantime there wasn't much to do but stay put. My body began to mend, but my imagination had time to dwell on things in earnest.

One night I woke from a late afternoon sleep, got out of bed, took two or three steps across the room, and halted in momentary amnesia. I had no idea who I was. I stood there in my underwear, becalmed, entranced by the blue prayerlike light filling my window, and then a few heartbeats later it all came back: the pain in my back, the peculiar tingle of mortality, shards of waking dreams that added up to nothing but the sense of being orphaned. I turned back to the bed, half-expecting to see a woman's body curled in the sheets, but there was no one at all.

I wandered across the hall to the bathroom, a narrow slot of a room with only a lidless commode. When I hit the light switch, the bulb flared and died. I sat on the can with only the last smudge of light in the dusty glass high over head. When I was done, I discovered that my key was twisted in the lock in such a way that the door would not open. I rattled the handle. Nothing. A strong cry might've summoned one of the other tenants of that dim corridor, but their ears were old and tuned a lot out, and, besides that, the hardware in my mouth let me only growl, like a groggy yard dog.

I sat down.

The darkness was complete. Minutes went by, and I didn't move, didn't holler, didn't lift my head. I felt perfectly severed, as though I had waked into a world I had always known would be there, a silent starless place where the species began and died in utter solitude, one by one by one. I thought of Johanna and Eric, saw their faces floating like reflections, the blackness shining through them. I knew I had not been brave in losing them, only stiff and sullen. I hadn't understood until now the truth of it: that I had not loved her, that I wasn't able to. I had wanted a family for comfort and retreat. All the times I had mumbled love in the dark were counterfeit. And she had known it first, known it pure and simple.

I had gone on and made a son and covered my lack of father feeling with an impatient, tin-faced act. Maybe it was true and good he would not remember me, maybe he would grow toward his own adulthood with only a strange hulking shadow lurking in the backwaters of his memory. Or maybe Johanna would turn up a big-hearted man who could believe a small boy's love was worth the world, and Eric would grow into such a man himself.

The sadness oozed around me like primeval silt. I was stuck in a closet stinking of mold and old men's urine and didn't care to free myself. I could blame myself, or not. I could curse the luck of the draw or the God I never knew. None of it mattered. The world takes it from you, regardless—even the thrill, even the energy to complain. There was nothing holy and nothing magical and no point believing it was a quest of any kind.

Shivering, in my Jockey shorts and faded Grateful Dead T-shirt, I started to cry, so hard it was more like a convulsion, every beat of it wincing up and down my backbone. Some time later I became aware of a pounding on the door and then the clicking of a key. It was then, for the first time, I saw Mr. Tornelli, his great head haloed by the red light of the EXIT sign across the hall.

"What's this?" Mr. Tornelli said.

I could say that Mr. Tornelli saved my life, but it wasn't right then, nor did the man seem a likely redeemer.

"Listen, Jack," he said, squinting into the cubicle, "You move your belly-aching out to the hall a minute, OK? I need the shitter."

In a moment I was in the world again, suddenly quieted. I didn't go back to my room but stood on the strip of balding carpet, waiting. Mr. Tornelli emerged after awhile, his eighty-year-old back a little straighter, his suspenders fastened, his collarless white shirt glowing in the weak light. His head seemed too big for the wickery body it rested on, and his moustaches—there were clearly two of them—were folded down over his mouth like wind-ruffled ptarmigan wings. Composed now, he studied me like a puzzle.

"You got pants?" Mr. Tornelli said.

I didn't answer.

He shook his head gravely. "Listen," he said, "you put your pants on and come down to my room. I'll wait right here."

A moment sometimes arrives when you see the different people you are and have been all at once. It happens without warning, the way a sudden shift of light will show depths in water. Before I'd gone into the bathroom I would have shirked the old man's offer, made a note to shun him in the halls. But I stood nodding at him, found myself pulling on my jeans and accompanying him to his room, the last one on the floor, the one next to the fire escape.

"You know this vertigo?" Mr. Tornelli said.

He walked slowly, both hands a little elevated as if holding imaginary canes.

"Afraid of heights?" I said.

He bent to hear my muffled voice. "No, no," he said. "Not afraid of high places. It's. . . . " He stopped and swiveled his head toward me and twirled his fingers in the air. "Feels like everything whirls."

"Bad," I said.

Mr. Tornelli smiled. "You get used to it."

Rooms at the Frontier were stark, unremitting. Out of superstition I had refrained from making mine any more attractive. Just passing through, the bare walls said. It was immediately clear that Mr. Tornelli didn't see it that way. His was bright and well-appointed: the bed was neatly made, covered with a star-pattern quilt; succulents and African violets and Wandering Jews were crowded on the desk by the southwest window; the walls were obscured by maps and star charts and color blow-ups. A giant photo-illustration of the full moon hung directly over his pillow.

Mr. Tornelli urged me to make myself comfortable. That wasn't possible, of course, but I eased into his straight-backed chair and looked at his little kingdom. He nodded matter-of-factly and sank into his white wicker rocker and folded his hands.

"So," Mr. Tornelli said, widening his great sapphire eyes, "you are a troubled boy and not in a good position to talk about it."

I tried to push the words forward with my tongue, a futile effort. Mr. Tornelli waved me off.

"Don't bother," he said. "You'll just swim around in it." He made an extravagant two-handed pulling motion. "Then you'll want a rope. Forgive me, but I'm not up to it anymore." He laughed with a kind of brittle pleasure. "When you get it down to one sentence, then I'll listen. Would that be all right?''

He rousted himself from the chair and went to the dresser.

''But then you won't need me, will you? No, for tonight's trouble the best thing is brandy,'' he said. ''Perhaps I should shoot it into your mouth with a syringe. Would you like that?''

So Mr. Tornelli and I drank the brandy. It worked on me as it does in the high timber, back to the wind. I stopped shivering. The cipher of ice in my middle began to melt under its heat.

I noticed after awhile that right above his chair was a brilliant photograph of a total eclipse: a golden ring shining around a black disk. Mr. Tornelli admitted having taken it.

''Kenya, 1973. Extraordinarily clear, no?''

I nodded.

''A good turnout that year, but blistering. Some of these young watchers are real zealots. It's good to see. I'll tell you, I spent most of my time under a beach umbrella. There was also, I remember, a type of flying ant that laid eggs in your hair.'' He threw open his hands. ''Ah, but I wouldn't have missed it. Over seven minutes dark. I had planned that it would be my last one, but maybe I was wrong.''

He smiled at me curiously. ''You know, I might live to see the one here.''

''Too many clouds,'' I managed to say.

''I know,'' Mr. Tornelli said. ''A bad season for the sun. But I think we might be fortunate that day.''

He stood, momentarily fighting the spinning in his head, then began giving me the guided tour: Caroline Islands, 1934; Boise, 1945; Manila, 1955; the Aleutians, 1963. A trajectory of blotted suns progressing across his wall.

''I hope you forgive me my fascinations,'' he said. ''Let me tell you a secret. I was born during the eclipse of 1900. My mother was crossing Louisiana on the train and stopped long enough to have me. Do you think I am a marked man?''

He laughed again, and for the first time in a long while I smiled.

''Do you know,'' he began again, ''*eclipse* means *abandonment?* It does. Abandonment. Can you imagine what it would be like if you didn't know about it? Everything's going along just like always, then *poof*, no sun. Imagine. You'd have some fancy explaining to do.

"The Ojibways thought the sun was going out so they shot burning arrows at it so it would catch on again. Another tribe thought all the fire in the world was going to be sucked up by the darkness so they hid their torches inside their huts. People have come up with a number of stories. . . ."

In the coming months the local papers would have a bonanza with the eclipse, playing science off legend. They told about Hsi and Ho, two luckless Chinese astronomers so drunk on rice wine they blew their prediction and were executed. They explained about coronas and shadow boxes and irreparable damage to the eye. In all I read I felt a strange longing for an ignorance that could make it crucial and magical. I thought about Mr. Tornelli's attraction, and it seemed that some of the raw amazement survived in him.

"We had a great friendship in those days," Mr. Tornelli said. "We would meet every few years, take in the spectacle and then go back where we came from. Never saw one another in between. It was all unspoken. Well, many of them are surely dead by now."

"Why are you here?" I asked him finally. It was the only important question I had for him.

"Why this fleabag? That's very good," Mr. Tornelli said, stroking the feathers of his moustache. "Where do you go when you can go anywhere? You think it matters? Well, I guess it does. To tell the truth, I knew a woman in this town once. A married lady, I'm afraid." He drifted a few moments. "Well, I remember how it was to be here and love somebody. Amazing, isn't it? Sometimes I ask myself if this was all the same life."

A few minutes past three, Mr. Tornelli finally stood again and insisted on walked me to my room. A comic, paternal gesture, it seemed. He said good night. Neither drunk nor sober, I lay in bed listening to the silence of the old hotel, the place the old man and I had come to. I imagined what it was made of: dentures soaking in a water glass, an old woman's dotted Swiss hanging in a closet with a lavendar sachet, dreams beginning and ending in some rooms and in others only the silence that follows the departure of one of our number. It was a powerful chord. I realized that Mr. Tornelli had done nothing except come between me and myself. Alone again, the trouble was with me. In the moments before sleep I tried to say its name in the simple sentence he wanted, but I could not.

Autumns here aren't the fiery poignant seasons they have in country with hardwoods and rolling hills. They are as abrupt here as the terrain. Indian summer vanishes overnight, clouds pour in from the northwest and smother the valley like dirty insulation. The rain comes quickly and strips the few maples and elms in a day, leaving the slick leaves puddled around their trunks like fool's gold. I woke late that next morning and a single look at the color of the light in my window told the story. My back had seized up overnight. It took many minutes to get upright, shuffle to the sink, and rinse the scum from my mouth with hydrogen peroxide. Mr. Tornelli seemed like a figment of last night's gloom.

I dressed carefully and went down to the pay phone and called Wayne at Workman's Comp. He sounded edgy. The computer in Helena had spit out my claim again. "Of course," Wayne said, "you know that *personally* I feel you're qualified. You know that, don't you?" I hung up on him and walked two blocks to the bank where the story was no better. Coming out I saw my ex-father-in-law heading toward the cafe. He speeded up to avoid me, then apparently thought better of it. He stopped and took me by the shoulders and gave me a good American once-over.

"You look like shit, you know that?" Darrell said.

"That's good news."

A logging truck rumbled past us, downshifting at the intersection, snorting black smoke in a long vibrant blast.

"How's that now," Darrell said, leaning in a little.

"I'd kick you down to the Feed & Grain," I said.

"No, you wouldn't," Darrell said. "You wouldn't do nothing. Boy, let me tell you, she had the angle on you all right."

He let go of me and shook his big pinkish head and walked off.

For weeks nothing seemed to change but the tiresome thaw and freeze of my back. When I could walk any distance, I scuffed through the town park, the sad remains of the founding family's estate, watching the ducks and Canadian honkers gather in the safety of the brackish pond. Mothers knelt in the cold grass behind their kids as they tossed wads of stale bread at the birds. I never had anything to give. Back at the hotel, I would sit on the edge of the mattress and feel the tightening set in.

I saw almost no one, except Mr. Tornelli. Days he didn't answer his door I went away undernourished, aimless, and vaguely dizzy. But most often he was there and ushered me in with a bright courtesy, as if he'd waited all day for me. He took my silence for granted. He talked freely, sprinkling the air with different voices. Sometimes I truly thought there were more than one of him. He had stared through the giant telescope at Mount Palomar; he had ridden boxcars from San Diego to the Midwest, once delivering the baby of a homeless woman in the light of a mesquite fire near the tracks; he had been an optics engineer at Polaroid. He had once been fired from a teaching position in Wisconsin for being a Communist, which he wasn't, and later asked to guest lecture as a blackballed scientist, which he declined. He had once shaken hands with Neils Bohr, the physicist, outside a hotel in Stockholm. He had taken peyote with Indians in a stone hogan in the mountains of New Mexico. In his vision he had become water, felt himself evaporating from the leaves of the cottonwood and rushing into the upper air and being blown high over the mountains with others like himself, then a great sense of weight and of falling at terrific speed through the darkness.

"Outstanding," Mr. Tornelli said. "I wish you could have been there."

I listened patiently. I came to suspect that his talks were something more than reminiscences, that they were aimed at me as if he knew the dimension and velocity of my mood. He always seemed to stop short of conclusions, though. The stories hung there, unresolved.

"Puzzling, isn't it?" he would say with a quick opening of the hands, as if he were releasing a dove, or maybe just giving up his grip on all that his mind had tried to bring together. I was entertained, diverted, moved.

Eight weeks to the day after Clevinger's outburst, the wires were removed from my jaw.

"So," Mr. Tornelli said. "Your tongue is out of its cage. A drink, to celebrate?"

"Thank you."

He handed me a gold-rimmed glass and retired to his chair.

"Now, maybe you can tell me about all this gloomy stuff?" he said.

"I think you know about it," I told him.

Mr. Tornelli leaned forward on his elbows, the light glowing on the waxy skin of his forehead. He looked at me a long time before speaking.

"There was a time," he said finally. "I was at sea aboard a freighter in the North Atlantic." He paused, as if squinting the memory into focus. "I couldn't sleep and there wasn't a soul to talk to. I went out and stood at the railing and stared at the ship's wake. My mind was empty, I could see nothing but the picture of my feet disappearing, then my shirt, my head, no brighter in the moonlight than a trace of the ship's foam. Let me tell you, I was *right there*. . . . "

"What was it?"

"Who knows? A bad time, a bad year. I was sick to death of my failures. I thought the world was a hopeless place. I stayed there all night, and then the horizon lightened a little, the wind came up, and I realized. . . . "

"What?"

He smiled lightly. "I was freezing. Freezing."

Other times he just let me in and returned to his chair and said nothing. As winter descended on us, these occasions seemed more frequent. The silences weren't painful, but it was those times that I could see him without distraction. Surrounded as he was by the battery of eclipses, the piles of spine-cracked books, *Scientific Americans*, fliptop steno pads filled with his faint ciphering, he seemed little and doomed. As he breathed, his ribs creaked like a ship's rigging. Sometimes he closed his eyes, battling the vertigo that spun fiercely in his head, fingering the gold medallion he wore around his neck. I finally understood that I had seen a man in his last brilliance. If my affliction was elusive and hard to name, his was as common as birth.

January was a menace. Days of cold froze the ground many feet deep and left anything exposed to the air brittle. Great clouds of exhaust drifted down the rows of pickups idling on the side streets, so thick they would hide a man. Steam rose to the ventricles of the top-floor radiators and we kept warm, the air in our rooms so humid we might have been in a sanitarium. Mr. Tornelli's plants flourished, but he seemed more and more unwell. His cheeks were smudged with shadows. I remembered how Johanna bent to the bedroom mirror smearing rouge on her face to invoke the same illusion. Mr. Tornelli was coming by it with a swiftness that prickled the darker chambers of my imagination. He had shown himself to be a man who took care of himself—with grace and dignity—but now I realized there were entire days he failed to eat.

I began escorting him around the block to a small restaurant that served steamed vegetables with its dinners. It catered to the nearby old folks home crowd, and there, in the midst of his peers, Mr. Tornelli nursed languid bits of Swiss steak and seemed to me for the first time no eccentric, no quaint loner. Sometimes I would catch him staring at the others and blinking.

"I don't know, Jack," he said softly. "Who are they?"

Midway through February the cold broke, and in the space of ten days the temperature rose fifty degrees. We could scarcely look at things for the sheen of the melting everywhere. As the date of the eclipse came nearer, I expected Mr. Tornelli's enthusiasm to rekindle. Surely he would muster some sort of celebration. He said nothing. I told him I could get a car and drive us up to Glacier Park, just the two of us. I told him I would help him get out his cameras again. He didn't want to talk about it. He was as short with me as I'd ever heard him. I backed off and waited.

The night of the 25th, Sunday, I went to his door convinced some excitement would show in him. There was no answer to my knocks. He had been sleeping irregularly then, so I swallowed my worry and left the hotel. The sky was streaked, but when I entered the darkness of the alley across the street I could see a few stars. Months ago he had known the sun would shine. I leaned on a dumpster behind one of the bars and stared up through a film of tears. A police car flashed its spot down the alley, and I recovered myself and went in and had a few glasses of beer, though the liveliness of the bar seemed desperate and stupid. It was almost midnight when I came out. From the sidewalk I could see the lights blazing in Mr. Tornelli's window.

I ran upstairs and knocked again and this time the silence was terrifying. I shook the doorknob hard against the deadbolt. I thought I was already too late. Finally I heard his voice, high and boyish.

"Are you all right?"

"Good enough," Mr. Tornelli said through the locked door.

"Could I come in?"

There was a long silence.

"Mr. Tornelli?"

"Jack."

"Right here."

"Could you let me be alone tonight? Would that be all right?"

"I want to be sure you're OK."

"Goodnight, Jack," Mr. Tornelli said with a queer force. I turned and went back to my room. I left all the lights on, thinking I'd get up in a few minutes and check on him. When I woke the sun was up, blasting gold off the windows of the abandoned Opera House.

It was after eight. The moon was already nearing the face of the sun. Still in last night's clothes, I ran down the hall and found Mr. Tornelli's door ajar. I walked in, but he wasn't there. The walls and bed and desk were stripped. A black steamer trunk sat in the middle of the floor, heavy and padlocked. Even the plants were gone.

I ran down to the desk and asked what was going on with Mr. Tornelli, but nobody'd seen him. I ran to the restaurant and stood at the end of the counter scanning the old heads bent over their poached eggs, but Mr. Tornelli's wasn't among them. Back at the Frontier I was desperate. I went up and down the corridor knocking on doors. He wasn't in the can. Mrs. Bache hadn't seen him. No one answered in 312. Mr. Karpowicz in 309 offered to break my jaw again. It was just after his door slammed that I saw what I had missed.

The door to the fire escape was propped open with one of Mr. Tornelli's African violets. The other plants huddled together on the metal slats of the landing. I turned and saw Mr. Tornelli's little medallion looped through the bottom rung of the old ladder that led eight steps to the roof. My heart pounded in my ears.

As I poked my head over the edge of the roof, the sunlight was growing gently dimmer on Mr. Tornelli. He was seated on half a hotel blanket laid over the moist tar and pea stones, cross-legged and tiny. This old man who knew the science of light, who had followed the shadow of the sun around the world, was at this moment sitting there staring naked-eyed into the eclipse.

He patted the empty spot next to him.

"Just in time, my boy," Mr. Tornelli said. "Sit please, keep me company."

I joined him on the blanket.

"Keep your eyes down now; don't ruin them," he said.

Darkness came over our part of the world in waves, stronger and faster now. The sparrows fell silent, the sound of tires faded from the streets below. The corona emerged brilliant from the black disk of the moon.

I took Mr. Tornelli's hand and held it in both of mine.

"I didn't know where you were," I said.

"Yes," Mr. Tornelli said. "You had to find me."

"I didn't know."

"So," he said, whispering, though in the stillness his words were bright and clear. "You see how it is with trouble and happiness. There are some good moments, aren't there. Were you asking for more than that?"

All at once the stars were everywhere, pelting their grace down on us.

"This is, ah, what can I say. . . . We come this far and you and I change places. It's good."

He shut his eyes, smiling still. I leaned over and drew his head down to my shoulder and stroked it as the breath labored in and out of him. The darkness began to ease; there was the slightest lightening visible at the edge of things.

Life As We Know It

That morning over shredded wheat St. John listened to the Blackfeet weatherman from Browning on the radio, then set out extra bowls of dried food. The cat looked down from the window sill where the lilacs, weeks past flowering, brushed the screen; she winked, dozed, her fur warming. St. John knew he'd need a few things before leaving, knew it was foolish to go all that way and have to compromise at the end. To train like a fighter and then lose because the last touch of polish had not been applied to the punch. He had coffee in the drugstore downtown where he was known as a regular, then walked down a side street to the antique shop.

The woman named Snowy stood at the counter reading the state weekly, yawning against the back of her hand.

"Well, if it isn't the king of glass doorknobs," she said.

St. John smiled, a man pleased by small tokens, recognition. He poked along the glass cases. Where the light from the street fell on the front of the shop, there was an order to the things for sale, almost frightening in its unattended regularity, but where that light failed in the rear of the store, there were things piled, a dark back room with furniture parts linked together in a heap. St. John thumbed a stack of circus posters and saw a framed picture of a monkey wearing a football jersey, number five, 1928.

"Something else I need today."

"I have it," she said.

"Rolls for a player piano. Old one."

"Take another step back and you'll trip on them."

"Nothing too battered. Nothing whorehouse."

"What kind of machine would they be for?"

"Jacobsen, Special Edition. Came out on the train before the turn of the century. Believe that? Call it mint shape," he said.

She opened the box for him. "Not a rip in there," she said. "Every one of those holes is cut perfect." He figured her for late forties, slim, a spray of freckles beneath her eyes.

"I'm sure they'll fit," she said.

"Well, I've got it right out in the truck."

"Oh? Where's she going?"

"L.A."

St. John pictured his truck again slipping into the weave of machinery on the freeways into the city. Then the slick facade of Recycled Interiors, Incorporated, and the alley, heavy with fried food, where he backed the truck in and unloaded his freight, his livelihood, somewhere over two thousand board feet of weathered Montana lumber: disassembled cabins, barns, sheds, broad-board fencing. In the new life they would decorate the walls of an insurance office, would spruce up the atmosphere of a postwar cocktail lounge striving to become a singles bar. Recycled Interiors. The square hole of a nail that once held a tin water dipper above a kitchen pump would stare down upon a world of mixed drinks and double-knit polyester; a freshly hatched Rocky Mountain arachnid would find itself sliding down a glistening avocado filing cabinet. At the incomprehensible rates per board foot, St. John knew it was more than an ordinary living. It was some kind of salvage rights.

"I was never in that state," she said.

St. John dug through a tin of buttons with the blade of his pocket knife. "You ought to. It's like nothing else." He picked out one that read State Exposition 1926 and pinned it to the flap of his denim jacket. "Figure this in," he said.

"Yeah," he said to the woman, "you ought to do just that. For a day or two anyway."

As an offer it resembled talk on the street about the long blistering heat they would surely have, the lack of rain, a constant.

"OK," she said.

"Huh?"

"You talked me into it."

St. John looked around the shop, and, finding nothing that would help, looked down into his hands. "You ought to know I drive this thing pretty much straight through."

"Lots cooler at night," she said.

St. John watched her walk the length of the shop and check the back door, her salt-and-pepper hair knotted and wrapped in a scarlet cloth at the shoulder, her thin legs moving as if she were parting tall grain with each step, precise and graceful as a sharpened scythe worked by supple wrists. She locked the glass front door and looked into St. John's washed-out blue eyes and smiled. She handed him the cardboard box of rolls.

"On me," she said.

It was a love of the used. A love he extended not to what was simply worn into an attractive, predictable old age, but to things that were first made well and, through some flirtation with the great mystery, had lasted. He looked out at the desert. As a child on the Hi-Line, a need for the long look had grown in him. Lying on baled hay as his father bumped the pickup over chuckholes, he had learned to appreciate seeing an entire storm welling up in the summer sky: the place in the west over the faint trim of mountains where it began and the other place beyond the town's dark buildings where it stopped and the blue sky that curved out over the borders to Saskatchewan and North Dakota broke loose. As he walked into the house behind his father, he would feel the first drops and watch them bang the standing dust into clouds.

St. John brushed crumbs from his lips. He looked over at the woman. "You ever gamble?" he said.

"Ned used to take me down to Jackpot sometimes." She spoke loudly, like a waitress setting down silverware too hard. "Had a good time mostly. Long time ago."

"Hell of a town. I nearly got shot there once."

"We went down on his weekends off. Last time he lost three hundred dollars and his boots." St. John remembered seeing blood spread through the white shirt of the man who'd been standing next to him at the bar, and the diving tackle over chairs and round tables another man had made for the waving wood-handled pistol.

"He bet his boots and he lost," she said.

She laughed.

"Just being married to him was enough gambling," she said.

"I guess you'd say I won though," she said. "He drowned just about the time I got sick enough of him to throw him out."

"That's a kind of winning," St. John said.

As he guided the truck through the eroding swatches of the first tarred road, St. John saw the gravel runway, planed and burning, where the interstate would be laid down. The flagman, a flourescent vest on his bare skin, looked at him.

"I think that sometimes," she said.

She pushed back a strand of hair, turning toward him. "One time he went on this *hunting trip,* know what I mean? Except I ran into one of his buddies on the street. . . . I mean the man didn't even have sense enough to get it straight with them."

St. John let it ride.

In his line of work St. John dealt with ghosts on a regular basis. You couldn't take down the place where people had lived or worked or stored their possessions or food for their animals without hearing their voices, one on top another or, sometimes, one all alone, low and repetitive. St. John was firm, and after awhile they understood something he believed: it was better for the wood to have another use than to rot away to nothing in the presence of grazing stock and magpies. It had preferences of its own. To the ghosts of men who had cleared trees or worked to buy mill lumber, it made a kind of sense. They argued for natural death, for dignity, but St. John was persuasive. "Things move on," he said. Also, they liked his singing.

"Hell, you don't have to be perfect," Snowy said.

The woman sat in the truck as St. John went into the office of the one-pump filling station. It was an old station, shaped like a large carport and made of cheap, adobelike concrete, the narrow original pump replaced by one that pumped regular, premium, and low-lead. The side of the building had been knocked out, and a white house trailer was attached to it and two trucks were parked by the other door. On the side of one of the trucks was a hand-painted sign that read SWEET LORD JESUS IS THE ONE I LOVE. St. John came out folding bills into his breast pocket. He was carrying a fifth of Lewis and Clark, swinging it by the neck.

"Terrible thing to get caught short in the wilderness," he said, pulling himself in by the steering wheel.

The first round she drank out of a Styrofoam cup that St. John found in the glove compartment and wiped out with his thumb, and after that she drank with him out of the bottle. She had slept through the worst heat of the day.

"Your radio work?"

"Too far out," he said.

She searched back and forth on the dusty band for a station that would stay clear. She gave up but left it turned on low.

St. John thought, forget that he had ever made this trip with other people. First, his brother Edgar who had started the operation with him when it had seemed like only a temporary scheme to buy into the antique market on the coast. They moved truckloads of tables and buffets and bed frames out of the small towns of Montana, until Edgar married two women in different cities. Until he eventually grew haggard in the violation of certain laws of time and space and migrated finally to New Zealand, a place said to be much like his home, only with an ocean. The habit of driving all night had begun with him. Also, the route, down through Salt Lake and across instead of straight through Nevada, because he liked to swim buoyed up in the big lake and drive through a city where fresh water, he said, ran continually in the gutters. A lot Edgar knew.

And forget that other women had gone with him one time or another. Try to forget especially, the night spent in the Sunshine Motel in Elko when the hitchhiker who had come on with him began to crash, and the prospect of a long night's roll with her became ludicrous before his eyes, like four tires going flat at once. She threw her guts up for an hour and sat in the room's only chair, sobbing, as St. John sobered; then, because he was there, she explained about running from the police who wanted her to testify against the man who had killed her boyfriend. Who had first taken movies of them and tortured her and then cut up her boyfriend and cemented him into the wall of a shower stall. Forget that.

Driving down the gentle slope of a basin where you could see maybe twenty miles across, St. John imagined he was riding an iceboat. He could feel the wind broadside the back of the truck, the pressure on his fingers against the wheel. Before him lay only sagebrush emptiness, perfectly articulated, a black track enameled across it. Go off the mark, he knew, and the ice will break quicker than rotten floorboards and you will disappear like a startled child into the boneyard of the American West. Or just run out of gas here sometime if you really want to feel like a man of the twentieth century. But on the iceboat it was not a question of fuel, it was a question of respect.

"What kind of name's 'Snowy'?" he said. "Ned give you that?"

"He had other things he called me." She was holding the bottle with the cap off and her thumb stuck in the hole. "No," she said, "that was from before."

"You were high-school snow queen."

"No."

"You could have been."

She sat with one leg folded under her, her free hand catching air out the window.

"My mother started it," she said after a minute. "I kept owls when I was a girl. They got to call you something when you're a kid."

"Sure."

"Well, it's better than 'Screech.' "

St. John laughed, and she laughed and looked at him and smiled to herself.

"When I'm an old woman," she said, "they'll think it's from my hair and I won't tell them any different. My mother got to be real old and white and they only called her Granny Wilder and one day I thought to myself: 'Well now, that's what it's all about, isn't it?' "

St. John drove the truck.

"And splitting myself up the middle two times wasn't exactly the best thing I ever did in my life, either. I couldn't ever see being a breeder."

St. John had heard how a middle-aged woman, a woman on the

verge of acknowledging an invisible line she had slipped over, can uncork. How she'll sit on a bar stool for an afternoon rinsing out her insides with alcohol and fruit juice mixed and then suddenly turn on a room full of strangers and begin dropping them with the indiscriminate birdshot of her life story. He had seen it. But Snowy was only talking as people talk across long stretches of land that does not seem in any way human, talking to a man who was a stranger, but through no fault of his own, only a stranger from a particular shifting perspective in time.

St. John listened.

The sun headed into the mountains straight over the highway and the desert shone gold. St. John pulled the truck over, and they waited, not talking, at a picnic table for the twilight to come on. A car passed. He lay with his cheek against the warm wood, and she worked with the heels of her hands on the spot near the small of his back that ached.

Snowy was sitting up adjusting her hair. The damaged Cadillac tilted on the shoulder of the road ahead was a shade of pink just slightly less believable than the clouds lingering over the mountains. Standing on the vinyl roof waving his arms, the old man named Milton could be seen a long ways off.

Snowy grinned at St. John. "A pioneer," she said. "They're not all extinct."

Milton was wearing a tuxedo, a new one, with mustard on the lapel. He looked more than anything like a freshly stuffed sage grouse, and he stunk, for no reason that St. John could lay hands on, of fish fertilizer.

"You got any idea what that god-blessed thing cost me? Cost me my damn life, that's what."

"This is Snowy," St. John said. Snowy's knees were pushed against the stick shift.

"Milton," she said, "drink some whiskey."

"Ma'am, I could just cry."

All his life, they learned, Milton had been the owner and proprietor of a hot springs. The baths could work surprising results, he said. Stomach troubles, chronic indigestion, kidney, bladder, and liver ailments, eczema, and assorted other complaints could be expected to be relieved. Limp in, hop out, he said. Milton cursed antibiotics. But, as he was no fool, he had seen it coming. At the brink of being, in every sense, too late, he sold all his land to a developer and went on the bus to Denver, where he bought new things until he got tired of doing that, and then took his remaining windfall, still substantial by normal reckoning, in a Super-Save sack and lit out for whatever the coast he'd never seen had to offer an old man with a bag full of money.

Milton handed the empty bottle back to her. She held it up to the windshield and looked at it.

"I'm obliged," he said.

"Under the seat," St. John told Snowy. "By your right foot."

Snowy pulled out a Boy Scout canteen.

"Terrible thing for a man to get caught in the wilderness," he said.

"Mister," the old man said, "I couldn't agree with you more."

St. John watched an animal shoot under the crossing glare of his headlights. On the northern roads it might be a deer, standing on the sandy shoulder, eyes glinting red the last moment before it bolted out into the fenders—or not.

"So you never been to Reno, then."

"Never did," said the old man.

"Well, that's where we're going. Snowy and I are going to do some gambling."

"We do it for a living," Snowy said. "St. John has the system. Right?"

"Don't need a system if you're a natural like this man here. Listen to me, Milton. You could have yourself one fine rip with that sack of bills."

"Can't lose it," Milton said.

"Relax, you won't lose it," Snowy said. "No way." She stretched her arms out across the seat in back of the two men where the leather was cracking like the bottom of a dried-up pond.

"You understand why a man like me needs this here. . . ."

"You could undo that tie," Snowy said. She reached over and

yanked it down like the string of a grain sack. "Look at this." she said. "It's a real one. How'd you tie that?"

"I ain't stupid."

St. John laughed.

"Ain't nobody's fool," said the old man.

"One thing," St. John said, "you never seen so many lights as there." That was how he thought of Reno himself. Since he nearly always passed through after dark, it seemed to him some vast instrument panel, each colored light blinking in a distant purpose all its own.

Milton worked on the Boy Scout canteen. He hummed. He beat time on his knee. "Cheap whiskey always reminds me of Ma," he said. He hummed. "When we got snowed in, I laid out in those springs all morning watching the steam rise and the snow fall. Then I'd go into the kitchen and she'd still be there with her coffee cup full of whiskey, and she'd kiss me with those big sloppy lips she had."

Snowy rubbed her fingers lightly along St. John's collar, looking through the weak light at the old man.

"Then she made me read out of the Bible at her. I'll tell you one thing right now, she couldn't get enough of those prophets. 'And a man shall be as rivers of water in a dry place.' That one was her favorite. 'That's us,' she said. Well, *bullshit.*"

Milton was humming what might have been "Nearer My God to Thee," his head keeping a side-to-side pace that lagged behind the tune part of a beat.

In the dark, St. John knew, the iceboat must be made to run on instinct. He locked the blades into an invisible track across the surface of the ice, knowing that now he would not need to interfere, only to watch for the unexpected. He remembered lying with his body stretched out, touching as many bales as he could reach, his brother doing the same, as they kept the truck's overload in balance. Snowy rested against his shoulder.

"Algae," the old man said. "Not one more lick."

Well past midnight, under the gentle guidance of house booze,

Milton lost his fear of spiritual poverty. St. John and the woman stood in back of him at the table where his chips were mustered in front of him like toy cavalrymen. The report from the front was favorable. Milton slipped chips into the barmaid's cleavage, kept winning. Then, without explanation, the boys in blue began to fall. Before it could become a rout, St. John nodded to Snowy and pulled him away.

"Let's go," he said. "You haven't seen the best ones yet."

Snowy helped him into the truck.

"When you get old as me. . . ."

"Mildew," St. John said, "Shut up."

"Just want you to know why I'm winning."

"I know why," St. John said. "Because you're a lucky old son of a bitch. No other reason."

Milton looked up sharply. "That's right," he said. "I'm a lucky old son of a bitch. That's right. But I took care of myself."

He laid his face over next to Snowy's, looking like a badly stuccoed wall. "Ain't that right?"

Snowy kissed his cheek. "You're a son of a bitch."

St. John started off through traffic. People walked out of the casinos in evening dress, walked in small groups past junk shops, storefront offices, and dry cleaners. St. John made a right at a corner where there was a gleaming all-night luncheonette.

"Stop this rig," Milton shouted. "Hurry, I'm an old man."

He slid out the door before the truck was stopped, hiked back down the sidewalk swinging the paper sack as ballast. St. John double-parked.

"You're right about one thing," Snowy said.

He pinched the bridge of his nose, looked over at her with a one-sided smile. He kissed her lightly, without lingering. She tasted vaguely like lilacs.

Milton stepped loudly onto the running board, motioning for a dark-haired girl in a long red dress to climb in.

"This is Michelle. She's coming with us."

St. John turned on the cab light and everyone looked at each other. Michelle smiled. She had teeth like kernels of sweet corn allowed to overripen on the cob.

"You're going to have to get up on his lap," he said finally.

"She's our luck," Milton said.

"You already got luck," St. John said. "Man as crazy as you should have been dead years ago."

Snowy stared at the girl who couldn't have been more than twenty. "You're the one that's going to need luck," she said to her. "All you can dig up."

"I won a TV," Michelle said. She was bouncing up and down on the point of the old man's knees. "Only we had to trade it for a rug."

St. John wondered briefly if Snowy's daughter would be this old, if she would be wearing a long red dress and smell like a drugstore. The towering sign of Harrah's whirled against the night sky. St. John turned down the Strip.

"Michelle and me are getting married," Milton said.

It is possible that the girl in the red dress thought that, in some not very complicated way, the old man was kidding. Or that her one prurient peek inside the old man's paper sack had been enough to set into motion a train of thought that had become, in a very short time, an express, in fact, the unlimited. St. John felt bizarre crosscurrents whipping his sails.

"Lord," Snowy said.

Outside it was somewhere between a reasonable hour of lateness and the uncompromising Reno dawn. St. John had begun to think of his recent hours of drinking as a stretch of deep foliage from which he was again emerging into light. He was perfectly willing to call the old man's hand.

"Well, you got all the luck tonight, my man," he said. "They have wedding chapels here that are open all night. Any time a fool like you gets the itch."

"Not any more," the girl said. "You want to get married after midnight, you have to go down to Carson City."

"Since when's that?"

"Oh, since they figured out Carson City needs the money. But you're right, they have the licenses and everything. Any time."

"You have experience in that line?" Snowy said.

"I live here," she said.

St. John grinned to himself like the driver of a getaway car. He nudged Snowy.

"Maybe we ought to just go on to the casino," Snowy said.

"No, ma'am. First we're getting married."

"Snowy and I'll stand up for you," St. John said. "I haven't done that since I stood for my brother the last time, and I wish I didn't then."

"I never did," Snowy said. "Of course, none of you fools have ever been to the line yourselves."

"I'd be obliged," the old man said. "OK with you if these kids stand for us?"

The girl looked at Snowy and pulled at her strap. "Sure," she said. "They're your friends."

St. John found the E. M. Percival Wedding Chapel on the outskirts of Carson City.

"Flowers," Michelle said, still in the vestibule. "I've got to have some flowers."

"Are you a justice of the peace?" St. John asked the small man, as he stood blinking in the amazing lime-sherbet light of the chapel.

"That's close enough," the man said. "We have the authority."

"Well, this girl needs some flowers if she's getting married," St. John said. "Something, you know, *tasteful.*"

In a moment the man produced an armful of plastic roses, both red and white, tucked beneath satin. "Here's what we have until morning," he said.

St. John looked at them, quickly pushed them at the old man's chest, suddenly aware that there might be something in the group's total appearance that could make any argument about style more or less beside the point. His mouth tasted like road tar.

The two women were talking beside the ring counter, one of Snowy's arms loosely over the girl's shoulder. What kind of advice would she be giving? St. John circled with his hands stuck into his high pockets, feeling like a ship's captain who has come to a port where the native customs seem dangerously out of the ordinary. Suddenly reluctant to turn over command. The old man had fallen silent.

"Milton," he said. "Go with this man and get the papers fixed, will you?"

Snowy crossed the small room, which St. John figured to be the original dining room of a house that had been converted to commercial use, like the funeral home in Great Falls where, not long before, they'd laid out his uncle. The ceremonies took place in the living room where there was an organ that nobody ever seemed to play. Snowy's blue smock was limp from riding. But, St. John thought at that moment, she looked somehow the least damaged of any of them. Her eyes were fresh.

"I got married in the Lutheran Church in Kalispell, and it rained all that week," she said.

St. John began to say something. The man stepped through the doorway and called in. "I think we're ready."

"Where's the old man?" Snowy said.

"He's not that old," Michelle said. "He went to the bathroom."

For the first time, St. John saw that she was not a bad-looking woman after all. Her dress was cut respectfully low, and a spot glistened between the tops of her breasts where she'd just touched herself with perfume. Milton walked up next to her, licking the corner of his mouth, then beaming, to all appearances a man delighted to be escorting his granddaughter to the Elks' Club Christmas Ball.

St. John felt hungry, cold spreading downward into his intestines. He realized that in some way he was deeply in awe of actual working craziness. He imagined how, in a few days, a tow truck would respond to a highway patrol call and and bring the old man's Cadillac in off the desert. It would stand in the sun next to the garage in a town like Lovelock, possibly for a long time. Possibly long enough for the attraction to wear off. Also, he thought as he watched the man show Michelle where to stand, a car like that could be stolen, could eventually, in a way not anticipated, make it to southern California on its own, fulfilling some kind of American legacy.

"Go on in," he said to Milton. "Just a second."

"Snowy," he said. "Let's all of us get married."

"What?"

"I want to marry you."

She looked at him, her back to the room where the others were waiting. She looked into her cupped hands.

"Nope."

"How come?"

"You could get a young girl like that if you wanted."

"That's no reason."

St. John looked at her eyes closely. In the hollow of her face they were like stones, blue-green sapphires set into rings that had survived more than a single generation.

"Snowy, I love you."

"It's OK," she said smiling, leaning forward against his chest. "It's OK."

St. John saw the desert again in his mind, felt the dry wind again. Soon the sun would rise at their backs. Snowy took his hand and kissed it, and he touched the back of her neck and held it, and it felt to him as cool and sleek as a marble swan.

Border Crossing

Carver drove. T.R. had told him they would switch off, but T.R. would rather give directions, and after all it was his trip. So Carver had driven since Colorado, and that was three days ago. It felt late to him, after midnight, and he didn't like being on this road. The car was junk, T.R.'s brother's Galaxie wagon—bad tires, a front end that floated, a car you could leave at the side of the road and not feel bad about it. They'd been off pavement over an hour, bearing north along the Flathead River's North Fork, aimed at one of the least-used ports of entry anywhere along the three-thousand-odd miles of Canadian border. April in Kay County, Oklahoma, was a decent season, but up in Montana, Carver thought, it was no good at all. The road was a hazard, deep holes and washouts, rutted with refrozen mud. Hard banks of corn snow rose luminous and spooky above eye level in places. Carver steered hard, every jerk of the wheel telling him not to count on anything.

Earlier T.R. had touched his man in Pueblo for nearly two thousand in cash—money owed him under circumstances never spelled out for Carver. He had also come away from that house with a Hillbilly Bread sack full of Colombian weed, a grab bag of pills, and some foil-wrapped grams of coke. T.R. had been high ever since. Carver drove hour after hour, listening to T.R.'s beautifully angry speeches—real good long-winded harangues against the powers that be, a world rigged with hassle. He heard the trip evolve in T.R.'s imagination from just another drive away from small-town Oklahoma, to something bigger, a quitting of America itself. It was exciting talk, and, while Carver wasn't one to show pleasure, he watched the empty landscape disappear past the curve of the windshield, happy to be once again caught up in T.R.'s plans.

But now that they were within striking distance of the border, Carver didn't have the sense of having crossed America at all. They were just roads. T.R. had quieted down, not apparently a sign of inner satisfaction, but of the energy it took to transform his rampaging thought into actual spoken words. He was bent forward on the seat, studying his maps with a predatory concentration.

"This thing don't say enough," he said, jiggling the flashlight to keep it lit. "Should of got one of those other kind with the lines on it."

T.R.'s wife, Clare, was passed out in the back seat. Carver could hear the air bubbling through her lips. She was thirty, a year older than T.R., a small, chunky woman. Her hair was fixed in red ringlets meant to be full and sassy-looking, but the car ride had left it stringy, and her face jutted out, its skin thin and bone white, sprayed with freckles like fine ash. Sometime earlier she'd told Carver to stop the car so she could throw up the remains of their last meal—chiliburgers and fries and beer in a cafe in Idaho when it was still light. Carver didn't look, but T.R. swiveled on his seat and laughed and called her a *Beauty*.

Clare did nothing for Carver sexually, but, then, women were a problem for Carver, too complicated and secretive. He wasn't even sure what to think about her being T.R.'s wife. In six years they'd only lived together a few months. She'd had three kids, and only one of them was T.R.'s—the middle one, Lonnie D.—the first coming when she was in high school and the last while T.R. was doing eighteen months down in McAlester.

Last night, out somewhere in the high plains of Wyoming, they had snorted the last of the cocaine. T.R. crawled in back with Clare and put down the seat and unrolled a sleeping bag. Carver's foot tingled on the accelerator. He turned on the radio and ran up and down the dial, nothing much coming in clear except some syndicated show of Bible songs, easier stuff to listen to than the squirmy sounds of T.R. pumping on his wife. Burl Ives sang "In the Sweet By and By." Powdered, heaven-scented sugar. Carver thought about their new life over the border somewhere out there in the stunted darkness. T.R. asked him if he wanted a turn. There was a silence, then he asked again, and Carver heard a slapping sound, but he couldn't tell which of them was hitting the other. It was all just a joke anyway.

Until T.R.'d sauntered into the office of the Spurs Motel where Carver was night clerk, Carver hadn't laid eyes on him for half a year. It was a stupid job, procured for him by his Aunt Ginger's latest flame, a local truck-leasing magnate named Chuckie Cyr. Still, it gave him a place to be at night that wasn't automatically trouble, and with the bum luck he'd had lately it wasn't so bad an idea. All he had to do was stay awake to check in the long-haul truckers and wake the salesmen early. It wasn't hard since he didn't sleep well at night anyway. He watched the cable TV until it went off at four, then read whatever newspapers people left on the chairs out front.

Carver still had a full year to run on his probation. He'd been busted—sale of dangerous drugs. It was a set-up. He never claimed he didn't do it, just that it wasn't any of his idea. But, as Ginger had said, *That's got nothing to do with nothing,* and when she talked Carver could not help listening.

Even now, he remembered distinctly the time when she was his only blessing in the world. His mother had been killed in a five-car winter wreck on the road to Tulsa the year he turned twelve. The job of mothering him fell to her sister, only twenty-three then, unmarried, an earnest, large-boned, dishwater blonde with Baptist leanings. She cried with Carver and told him how much she grieved for his mother, too, then settled him and went about raising him like it was her personal mission. Or so it seemed.

Carver's mother had always said his father died before he was born—hinting at tragic circumstances he'd understand when he was older—and that was what he believed until one day out of the blue Ginger told him otherwise. "That was just her way of putting things," Ginger said. "He was more on the order of a fling. Your mother was a very *popular* lady." For the first time Carver picked up on the fact that Ginger had an abiding jealousy of her sister, that her love for Carver was laced with resentment and a blooming notion of her own failures. Carver didn't understand it well, but he felt the tension, more open and troubling as he grew to high-school age.

The night T.R. presented himself at the motel, Carver was standing by the wall-mounted TV. The vertical hold was on the fritz, and there was nothing he could do to hold the image in place.

"They got good color sets in the rooms," he said blankly to T.R., the first words between them in six months.

T.R. was already fired up. Grinning, he cuffed Carver on the shoulder. "Richard," he said. "You're my man, right?" T.R. was the only person who ever called him by that name. T.R. made it sound important. He thought maybe his mother had called him *Richard* sometimes, too, but it was difficult to recall exactly.

"Hey," T.R. said. "Right?"

Carver turned from the flipping picture and nodded. Inside five minutes T.R. had made a shambles of Carver's desire to play things on the safe side.

There was something about him that Carver could not stay clear of. He had five years on Carver, enough to be a good older brother, but it was never like that between them. Carver had known him as long as he could remember, first only by the reputation he left behind in school—a kid with a quick pair of hands and a loose mouth—and later, when their lives brought them together in town, Carver recognized in T.R. many things he lacked in himself. T.R. knew who his enemies were. He didn't scare. He never seemed brooding or depressed, the way Carver was so often, only angry for specific reasons and hell-bent on getting even. This was countered by a good strong smile and a manner of talking that made anything seem like it could be done. Carver never seemed to mind the fact that T.R's various traits didn't add up to much of a whole. What he liked was just being around T.R. because then he would not need to agonize over decisions. T.R. was happy to make them all.

Though Carver had been sticking close to home lately, the grapevine had told him of T.R.'s run-in with the sheriff. The charge read *grand theft auto,* but rumor said the car was not so much stolen as borrowed, T.R. being the object of a grudge. All of which was not an especially big deal in itself, but with T.R.'s record it added up badly.

He came to the point quickly, or to part of it, anyway. That afternoon he'd skipped his hearing, and there was every reason to think it would be a good idea to leave town. He had business in Pueblo and would Carver like to come along for the ride? Much later Carver wondered why he had been so willing to walk out of the motel, and all he could think of was that it hadn't sounded like much of a question. As Carver was retrieving his jacket, T.R. looked over at the exposed cashbox, then, catching Carver's eye, let it be, and they walked out together.

They drove to a cinder-block lounge at the west edge of town, and T.R. told him to pull up and wait. He went inside and came out alone in a minute and stood by the corner of the building. Carver could see the blue neon flashing off the side of his face. Carver was cold in the car, but T.R. was outside in only a T-shirt and short denim jacket, unsnapped. He looked ever harder and more stripped down than Carver remembered. Carver had sometimes seen T.R. with his clothes off, and it always made him feel blubbery and out of control and halfway ashamed of himself.

Clare stepped out and talked to T.R. He had been in and out of Ponca City so often that year that she and the kids had moved back in with her mother. Carver had heard she was divorcing T.R. She rested her shoulders against the wall as T.R. leaned over her. They were out of earshot, but Carver could see her shaking her head, slowly, as if weary of what she heard.

T.R. came back, and Carver asked him what they were doing; T.R. smiled and put a finger to his lips. Soon the back door opened, and Clare slid in and they drove away. They stopped for no more than ten minutes at her mother's house while she got out of her uniform, and then they were on the road out of town.

Why would a woman take off with a man she was divorcing? Some brand of female nostalgia that was beyond him, Carver thought. It turned out that T.R. had told her they were going to Mexico, had sold it as a spring run. T.R. had led her there once before, another spur-of-the-moment trip five years past—the end of some events that had included T.R.'s having punched Clare's father senseless during a Sunday dinner. That time they made it all the way to the Pacific beaches and didn't come back until T.R. caught hepatitis, his wide-set flashing eyes soured by jaundice, his ankles so swollen he could scarcely move without Clare's help. No, Carver didn't understand Clare at all. When they turned north in Pueblo, she only sat in back and was quiet. It didn't occur to him until much later that in a life like hers, north and south amounted to the same thing.

Now through the moonlit clearings Carver saw the peaks of the northern Rockies, close at hand and gleaming like the jawbone of a wild dog. He'd stopped drinking hours ago, but he could still feel the rustle of amphetamine in his bloodstream. He was driving round-shouldered, two hands on the wheel, having a hard time deciding what anything was. He thought he saw a coyote trotting along beside the road, its eyes fixed on him in a bright leer. But it wasn't there, nothing but fallen timber and the angle of moonlight.

T.R. grabbed his shoulder. "Jesus, Richard, wake up. I said *turn.*"

Carver took his foot off the gas. "What?"

T.R. pointed to a side road. "Reconnaissance."

Carver swung the car around and drove slowly down through a swath of aspen to a clearing spotted with log buildings, all dark except the sheen on their steel roofs. The largest had a tall false front with turn-of-the-century lettering that said MULLAN'S CROSSING MERCANTILE. The glass was dark. As they passed, T.R. looked at the padlocked gas pump out front, then leaned and squinted at the car's gauge, which was hovering a little above half.

The road curved down past a row of trailers and sheds. In the fields beyond, a dozen or so horses were grazing, smooth dark shapes giving off clouds of breath. One lifted his head and stared at the car, chewing slowly.

"That's the way to live, huh, Richard?"

The horse took a few careful steps toward the barbwire, then stopped, watching T.R. intently for a long moment. T.R. broke off his gaze. "Don't look like this goes anywhere," he said.

Carver pulled into the only plowed driveway and started backing the Galaxie around and ran its fender into a hard berm of snow. The car slid, and the back wheel settled into a rut, hub-deep. Carver accelerated, but the car only wiggled sideways. The angle was bad. The more he tried to rock it, the more it slid and settled in.

T.R. reached back and shook Clare, then eased her upright by the hair. Carver got out, and the air straightened him up a little. He smelled the burnt rubber and could tell they were stuck good. Through the back window he saw Clare climb into the driver's seat, shaking the curls from her face. T.R. joined him at the bumper and they pushed, the tires spraying them with gritty mush.

"All right, enough," T.R. yelled. "This ain't doing nothing at all." He folded his arms and scanned the area. At the end of the long drive there was a pickup and a tractor with a plowblade.

"Go down and see if anyone's there," he told Carver. He shook his head at the car. "This trash," he said.

"What do you want me to say?" Carver asked him.

"Use your brains," T.R. said. "And take this."

Carver stuck the gun in his jacket pocket where it didn't quite fit, then into the waistband of his jeans where his soft stomach pressed on it. He walked down the drive toward the trailer. It was as far away from T.R. as he'd been for three days. He checked the pickup for keys, but there were none. He saw woodsmoke blowing faintly from the chimney pipe above the trailer. This was no fancy double-wide: it was old and round-cornered and grown-over with eccentric plywood and tarpaper additions. Carver walked slowly around the side, stood on a hay bale, and looked in.

Through the dark of what he supposed was the bedroom, he could see part of a couch in the front room, a hooded light illuminating a pair of hands that held a knife and a long chunk of yellowish wood. The man was carving an Indian head, it appeared, the knife twisting and slivering down the side of the neck, again and again in a cautious rhythm. Carver felt sorry he was going to have to interrupt. He jumped down and moved the gun inside his shirt and zipped the jacket.

He rapped his knuckles on the aluminum door and stood shivering in the entryway, the stink of boot preservative and oily wood strong in the dark. He knocked again, and a light came on by his head. He backed up squinting and read the blue plastic punch-tape lettering by the door. *Purdy Hoag.*

Hoag opened the door and looked at Carver as if he thought the pounding was only a trick of the mind. He was taller than Carver expected, and older, somewhere over seventy, he guessed. He had a blue plaid bathrobe on over his clothes. His forehead was high and round as a china bowl, the veins running up his neck like darkened flaws in the finish.

"Don't know you, do I?"

Carver shook his head. There was something spooky about the man, and he wished he could back away and leave him alone. Instinctively he recognized a look he saw on his own face many nights when he was able neither to sleep nor take part in the world either.

"Got ourselves stuck in your driveway," Carver said finally.

Hoag motioned Carver in, the knife still in his hand. "Well, I guess I'm your man," Hoag said, his face brightening. "If you'd of come along yesterday it would of been no good, but I got that tractor running again this afternoon. It won't be no trouble now."

Caught up in T.R.'s thinking, Carver had expected more resistance; still, he was pleased he could do his part so simply. The way the man talked explained something about how the people up here acted. "Yeah, that would be real good," Carver said softly. "Then we could just get going."

"Headed back into town tonight then?"

"Going to Canada," Carver said and immediately wished he'd kept his mouth shut. He knew he was always saying either too much or too little.

Hoag shook his head. "Somebody mis-explained it to you. This border ain't open at night."

Carver fidgeted. "Maybe there's some other way?"

"I wouldn't mess with it," Hoag said, folding himself slowly into a chair to lace his boots. Carver looked around the trailer, at the walls lined with old-time logging photos, and Hoag's carvings everywhere—buffalo and deer, Indian warriors with long feathered headdresses. Otherwise the place looked kind of greasy and solitary, Carver thought.

"Well, we'll just get that rig out and see what's what," Hoag said, more or less to himself.

"Sure," Carver said.

T.R.'s head was stuck through the passenger window. He was yelling at Clare, who knelt on the back seat, holding T.R.'s other pistol to her head and clicking her tongue.

". . . me the goddamn gun," Carver could hear. "Straighten up!"

She threw it past him and slumped back to the bedding. T.R. picked the gun up and tried to get the snow crystals out of the barrel with his little finger, then with a twist of T-shirt. Far behind him Carver heard the tractor's engine firing.

"There's kind of a problem," he said and told T.R. about the border.

T.R. didn't look surprised. He seldom did. He tightened his lips and stared over Carver's shoulder at the man approaching on the tractor. "That's OK," he said. "I was thinking these Okie plates might draw us a search anyway. I was thinking of taking the horses. That would be a good way to do it." He squinted in at Clare, then turned back to Carver. "Listen, what's this guy's trip?"

"Old man named Purdy," Carver said. "Just this old guy who hangs out up here and carves things."

"Shouldn't be no trouble?"

Carver shrugged.

Hoag brought the tractor up to the Galaxie and climbed down. The engine shook and misfired. He dug around in the box back of the seat and dragged out a length of heavy-gauge chain.

"Missed your turn, eh?" Hoag said. "I done it myself more than once."

Carver took the chain and got down on his knees and looked for something to fasten it to and ended up wrapping it around the front bumper. The radiator smelled hot, even in the chilly air. It was a dangerous, chemical smell. A wave of dizziness passed through Carver. Behind him, Hoag was asking T.R. how they'd happened down that road in the first place.

"Just tourists," T.R. said.

Hoag started to ask something else, but T.R. cut him off. Carver stood quickly and secured the chain to the tractor, and when he looked up he saw the last bit of a look that had just passed between T.R. and the old man. Hoag stared back at his house for a moment, then returned to the seat of his tractor and sat up tall, waiting, the car to his back. Carver thought he must look just like this out plowing after a storm, all alone, as barren and straight-backed as these trees.

T.R. stood back out of the way as Carver got in the car to steer. The slack snapped out of the chain all at once, and Clare rebounded off the back seat to the floor. Getting up, she flung her arm over the front seat, her long fingernails catching Carver's ear. He flinched but didn't turn to look at her. He kept the wheels straight and stared ahead, wishing he could just put his head down against the wheel until it was light.

When he got out, he saw Hoag bent to the chain where it met the tractor. He saw T.R. bear in on him fast, the butt of the pistol visible as it came down toward the old man's head.

But Hoag had already begun to rise and the blow missed the flush part of the head, only startling him and knocking off his hat. He straightened up to full height, his face glowing red in the tractor's taillights.

T.R. jerked back and drew down on him, two-handed, FBI-style. *"Goddamn,"* he said to Hoag. "Don't say a goddamn word, don't say nothing. *Richard. . . .*"

Carver joined him. T.R. had moved so fast that it was only now Carver saw precisely where things stood. He reached in his shirt and drew out his own gun and pointed it at Hoag.

"That's good," T.R. said. "Terrific. Don't let him move."

T.R. went back to the car and pulled open Clare's door and yanked her out by the arm.

Hoag didn't move, didn't say a word. He watched Carver carefully, his jaw grinding slowly as he chewed on his lip.

The trailer seemed too full with all of them in it. T.R. made a quick check of the bedroom and bathroom; back in the front room he noticed the Buck knife lying on the table by Hoag and nodded at Carver to remove it.

"You don't need no temptation," T.R. said.

Hoag's hands were folded in his lap now, his eyes upturned, watery and distantly yellow. Carver had gotten no farther than the door, the gun pointing down at the peeled-back linoleum.

"All right," T.R. said. "We're going to get this straight now," as much to himself as to the others. Hoag was frozen, no particular emotion showing except a slow watchfulness Carver took for fear.

"Go make some coffee," T.R. said to his wife.

Clare did as she was told, moving flat-footed around the kitchen, leaving a trail of open drawers and cupboards. T.R. pulled out a kitchen chair and turned it around and sat on it in the middle of the room where he could see everything.

"That bottle," he said in a moment. Carver fetched it over to him, a half-empty fifth of Jack Daniel's.

"You want a glass or something?" Carver said.

"This is fine here," T.R. said. He drank and extended the bottle to Carver.

"I don't feel like it," Carver said. "Maybe he's got a beer."

"Go see."

Carver opened the man's icebox and found four cans of Rainier on a plastic holder.

He thought maybe he was hungry, but he didn't want to eat anything. He didn't even really want the beer, but he thought maybe one would settle his nerves. Clare was watching from the sink as the water ran, not so much him as his movements, as if they were just something to focus her eyes on.

"You want one of these?" Carver said to T.R. T.R. took one but didn't open it.

"Give *him* one," he said.

Hoag took a beer and drank from the can carefully, relaxing a little as he did.

"Those are your horses?" T.R. said.

"Some are."

"Where's the gear?"

"You ain't that near to the border." Hoag said. "You won't make it in the dark. It will be light, and that's if you know what you're doing, which it doesn't look like."

T.R. smiled. "You're a helpful guy, Purdy. Where's the saddles?"

The beer felt sour in Carver's stomach. In fact, now that he'd been standing a while, he realized he hurt all over, a dull ache, as if all the padding between his bones had worn thin from jostling in the car so long. He wasn't drunk, and he wasn't sober either. He felt like he'd been sprayed with clear lacquer. The lights were too bright, but he knew if he closed his eyes all he'd see would be a straight slash of road and two headlights dovetailing into the darkness.

"All I'm saying is the way things are," Hoag said. "You don't come from around here so you don't know."

"Save it," T.R. said.

Clare brought in the coffee in two plastic cups. T.R. shook his head at her. "It's for you," he said. "Keep drinking it until you straighten up good."

Now T.R. was quiet, staring over the chair back at the old man, drinking from the bottle, now and then flicking his eyes up like a set of high beams to see if Clare was behaving herself. Carver leaned on the door frame, thinking about how he would send Ginger a postcard once they got to Canada. He wondered if Ginger had ever seen mountains like these. Before this Chuckie guy, she'd talked about marrying a man from Galveston and then she would have seen the water at least, not the ocean but something big enough. He knew it was all talk. She'd be working at the dry cleaners in Ponca City until the day the fumes finally rotted her brains out. *You get what you pay for in this life,* Ginger was fond of telling Carver, but he guessed it was just good advice, something to stick on a plaque, and nothing either of them took personally. Maybe he would skip the card. She'd be sore about the motel job, and he probably wouldn't know what to write on it anyway.

T.R. was up now, alert and grinning darkly, as if something he'd been waiting for had happened—an alignment of private tumblers. Carver loved that look. It made him feel a good deal better.

"You together now?" T.R. said to his wife.

"Don't I look wonderful?" Clare said. "Don't I look like your best old lady?"

"At least," T.R. said. He took Carver's gun out of his hand and gave it to Clare. "Here's what's going to happen. Him and me are going to go down and get the horses fixed up. You keep him just like that. Sit down at the table and drink your coffee, and don't let him do nothing at all."

The horses were pack stock, strong and well-broke and not spooked by strange men on their backs. Their breath was slow and salty. T.R. crooned nonsense to them as he patted their long faces and slipped in the bits. Carver stood by, wishing he had gloves and a decent coat, goosedown or buckskin with a heavy fur collar. He hugged a saddle blanket around himself and watched T.R. disappear into the shed with a lantern.

Beyond the corral was a line of cottonwood, a scattering of last year's leaves reflecting moonlight. Back home the willow and aspen were already green in the sloughs beyond Ginger's house, the buds splitting in day-long sun. It was like another country up here. He could hear the river moving beneath the cutbank, a steady restless sound rising from the thick shadows. He buried his chin in the blanket and sat waiting. He could not get warm. Shivering, his head down, it seemed as if the cold was coming from within himself.

He wished he could put Ginger out of his mind. He never could. She had trapped him as secretly as the town itself. He'd always known there was life beyond her, beyond the scruffy edges of the town, where the drive-in movie screen and the clustered stacks of the refineries stood like monuments against the freshening sky. The attachments were ingrown and confusing. He couldn't see past Ginger to his own mother. Their faces mingled, and the photographs Carver saved loose in an old Justin boot box only made him hurt and did nothing to explain how he should feel and what would be the right thing to do.

One night when Carver was sixteen he'd fallen asleep on the couch after watching Johnny Carson. When he woke, the TV was snowy and Ginger was standing in its light, watching him strangely as though she'd been there talking to herself for a while. Carver remembered she'd been out to the country club and had told him not to freak out if she stayed out all night. Earlier Carver had sat on the back porch and smoked a joint that somebody had given him and that he'd saved in his wallet for over a week. He'd gone back in the house and examined himself in the brightly lit mirror and decided it hadn't done anything but redden his eyes.

Now Ginger was sitting on the edge of the cushion, and he could see how puffy and streaked her face looked. She cleared the hair from his eyes and touched his face in a light, distracted way, shaking her head slowly.

"What kind of man are you going to be? Tell me."

Carver thought she was probably drunk. He didn't dare move. Her dress was slippery, scented with gardenias and smoke and fatigue.

"Don't you be one of those dumb bastards," she said. "One of those boys who never grows up."

Carver thought she was going to cry, but she didn't. He wanted to reach out and do something, but he was afraid of her and afraid of his own clumsiness. If he'd moved then, it might have all come out diffferently, but, as it was, the moment passed and the pitch of Ginger's mood changed. She bent and kissed him, not on the cheek as she sometimes did, but on the lips, holding her hand behind his neck, a patient, sleepy kiss. By the time it was over she had undressed him and crawled over him, all the time talking like it was a lesson, like they were conspiring against the way men acted. It was only when she finished with him that she cried, and Carver, his body blasted with adrenalin, his thoughts racing, didn't know what in the world to say, so he said nothing. She grabbed him by the biceps and dug her nails in and screamed at him, "Can't you at least talk to me? A few lousy words after all I do for you. . . ."

After that Carver didn't know what to expect. The next morning it was business as usual, Ginger flying around the kitchen late for work, her recital of things for Carver to do after school not diminished, nor anything in her voice betraying a change of heart. Though he was confused and had no one to confide in, the memory gave Carver a secret pleasure. For whole dreamlike moments, he felt the sweet danger of Ginger's attention on him; then he would shake the image from his head and try to concentrate on what he was doing, most often his thoughts then drifting into a more general sense of dread.

A few weeks later she again interrupted his sleep. She slid under the covers of his bed and began to speak to him about his *responsibility* to her. By that age Carver had begun to see that certain things happened out of the blue—acts of God, his mother had called them. Responsibility was something else, and Carver had only vague glimpses of what his responsibilities were. That night he settled for pleasing Ginger, hoping deeply, even as his body tensed against hers, that this was only one of those first things, that it might never happen again and was nothing he was required to understand.

"What's the matter?" T.R. said. "You cold?"

"Kind of," Carver said.

"You got thin blood, you know that? You ought to take vitamins or something."

T.R. flopped the saddlebags over the last horse and checked the cinches. He mounted his own horse, the tall dark one they had first seen at the fence.

Carver followed T.R. up the slope, leaning forward in the saddle as the horse stepped through the crusted snow. When they reached the top of the rise, T.R. turned toward the row of cabins and trailers that stretched down the flat away from Hoag's. They were all dark and showed no sign of recent use. The drifting snow had left wells around them on the sheltered sides. T.R. moved to dismount. Then a funny look crossed his face, and he pulled the reins around sharply and told Carver the outfitting would have to wait.

Clare had dropped off again, her cheek resting on the gun. Hoag was slipping across the room to make a grab for it when T.R. banged through the door, followed by Carver. Hoag froze. Another two steps and he might have made a stand. He backed to the couch and collapsed. While Carver kept an eye on him, T.R. kicked the table leg and Clare's head jerked upright, her eyes floating in a broken reverie.

T.R. backhanded her across the bottom of her face. Her head flapped against the paneling, a streamer of blood running from her split lip. Carver turned away.

"What shit is this?" he could hear T.R. say, the last bit of patience gone from his voice. "I can't leave you alone ten minutes?"

Chairs scraped along the linoleum. Clare was trying to talk, but the words were muffled by her effort to breathe. Carver saw Hoag staring at him, as if they shared something.

"You shouldn't of done that," he said to the old man. "I guess you had to try something, but you should of not."

Hoag kept looking, gnawing on his bottom lip. Carver didn't like it. Old men gave him the willies, especially this one, the loose splotchy skin hanging from his jowls, the soft puckering around the eyes. He didn't want to have anything in the world in common with him. He wanted to be down the road, already beginning to forget the insides of this trailer, its shabby smells, all those carved faces staring down.

Carver heard water running, looked up to see T.R. holding his wife's head under the tap. In a moment she shook free and twisted away from him, grabbing Hoag's blue bathrobe to wipe herself.

"You with me now?" T.R. said.

When Clare didn't respond, T.R. looked at Carver, then at Hoag. "This here is going to take all of us together. All right? This close and I don't need anyone messing me up. Clare, honey, you following me?"

The hurt had already disappeared from Clare's expression, replaced by a pouty indifference.

"Richard?"

Carver nodded.

"Watch him good," T.R. said, returning the gun to him. I'm taking her out to get some things, then we'll go. Think about if you need anything."

The door slammed behind them and the trailer was quiet. Carver began to picture the loaded horses walking along the river, T.R. up front, Clare in the middle, and him in back trailing the pack horse. He imagined there would be no talking, only the click of hoofs on smooth stones, the snow's crust cracking, the pleasant creaking of the tack. By the next night they would be far enough into Canada to sleep. They would shoot something and roast it over a fire of deadfall and make plans. Carver couldn't picture it much past that. He slipped the gun back into his waistband and poured himself some coffee and sat down across from Hoag just as T.R. had sat.

After a few minutes he asked Hoag if he wanted anything. Hoag shook his head.

"You're not going to try anything now, are you?" Carver said. "I'd rather if we just sort of waited." He blew steam off his cup and drank, feeling the heat all the way down. "We'll be gone pretty soon and you can forget all about us."

Carver didn't expect an answer but Hoag said, "You see those pictures up there?"

Carver gave them a glance. Loggers posing with their great-toothed saws beside massive felled trees.

"You have any idea what kind of work that meant? You can't imagine it. I mean real all-day work. I've been coming up here forty years and a lot's changed, but some things are pretty much like they was, and one of them is nobody's going to forget you right quick." Hoag rubbed his face, then his head where he'd been struck. "I'm telling you it's shameful to prey on a man who stops to help you."

"I'd rather if you didn't talk that way," Carver said.

"I could always come away to this place," Hoag said. "It's how I stayed married to one woman so long. I don't doubt but it looks like trash to you, but that don't matter, you see, because I know the worth of it. I could always come here and keep from hating her. Now it's the only place I have. You get bear sometimes. But bear and the hard snow and summer fires is just part of how you figure it, just part of what happens."

Hoag stopped, then added, "We never had no hoodlums come up here."

"T.R. wouldn't like to hear you talking like that. He can be kind of touchy about things."

"That's just fine," Hoag said. "Because I'm talking to you, not him. I was saying we get our share of trouble and craziness. Sometimes a husband or a wife will get a bellyful and you have a shooting, sometimes a man will take his truck out in the woods and put the gun to his own head. I don't mean I admire any of it, but a man can understand it, you see?"

Carver wanted to assure Hoag that he wasn't about to shoot him, but he couldn't give up his advantage, nor could he let himself show how nervous the gun made him.

The summer Carver was sixteen, not long after life with his Aunt Ginger had taken its strange turn, Carver had done a favor for T.R. It involved the storage of stolen weapons—largely military, driven upstate from Fort Sill. Carver wrapped them in burlap and stuck them in the empty pig shed behind the house, sometimes going out to look at them, squatting back in the doorway and sighting down the barrel over the sloughs and weeds toward the rolling grassland where he often walked that summer. Holding the cool gun metal, he remembered the TV pictures of the returning GIs. He looked out at the land and tried to imagine taking enemy life. It was beyond his understanding. He rewrapped the guns, and in a few weeks T.R. came and took them away, explaining they were part of a deal and nothing to shoot. But T.R. had kept one, an automatic, had used it that Labor Day to hold up the 7-Eleven out on Route 77, firing a burst across the beer coolers as he left, the chunks of frosted glass flying across the floor so fast the clerk had no time to shield his face. T.R. called that part an accident.

"Still," Hoag went on, "there's a lot I don't understand. Maybe I wasn't meant to, but you know a man has a need to figure things out, especially things that don't fit with the rest."

Carver got up and looked out the window, shaded his eyes from the light. The yard was quiet. He could see the back end of the car and two of the horses tethered to the bumper.

"Like it was with my wife at the end. You wouldn't of wanted a better wife than she was, full of sauce, you know, but when she got sick all the fight went out of her. She just laid there until it killed her, couldn't seem to do nothing to help herself. You understand? Wouldn't do a thing."

"Sure," Carver said. "Listen, I think it would be good if we just sort of waited, you know?"

"And I've been trying to figure out what you boys are going to do up in Canada."

Carver shrugged. "It's going to be better, that's all."

"Better than what?"

"This life here," Carver thought. He looked at the floor, flushed with the sudden desire to explain himself. "It just got *bad* somewhere. People just screw you and screw you, one thing right after the other. Even your own people end up hassling your head until you can't hardly get a decent breath. It's like. . . ."

Carver stopped abruptly. These were T.R.'s words—but he didn't know what else to say. T.R. could keep it going for hours, it seemed like, and it would all come out right.

"What I mean is," Hoag said, "what *exactly* are you going to do? What are you going to do Monday morning?"

"That don't involve you, does it?" Carver said.

"No, I suppose not, once you get across the border. Except you'll still have my horses. Used to be they shot horse thieves."

"I wouldn't say we was horse thieves," Carver said.

"No," Hoag said. "Horse thieves at least know what they're doing. You three are just some low-life trouble from someplace else."

Carver wanted very much for T.R. to be there and take over. "Those Canucks are good people and don't hassle you," he said, but it sounded lame, even to himself.

Hoag smiled for the first time. His sparse brows rose into crescents, his eyes moist and blinking. "You're a awful fool," he said. "This is no country for fools."

Carver tried to pinch away the pain between his own eyes.

"Especially a fool with a gun. And let me tell you something else, boy. . . ."

"I don't want to hear it," Carver said. If he had a moment's peace, Carver knew he could figure out what he should think. He felt himself slipping. The only power he had over Hoag was what he could accomplish with the gun, which was nothing without the will to fire. The less Hoag knew about him the better—but he had the feeling that Hoag knew too much already.

Still, when Hoag had been quiet for a while, Carver asked him what it was.

"No," Hoag said. "I'm just going to save my breath."

Jesus, Carver thought. He checked the window again but found nothing changed. He wished he'd taken a leak earlier. He didn't want to hassle tying Hoag up himself. If T.R. didn't come back soon, he would have to go in Hoag's sink.

The old man's gaze had turned baleful. "You could let me go now," Hoag said.

Carver looked at him. He was sorry the man had said that. His job would be easier if they both tended to business. He was even a little offended.

"Wouldn't it be better if you just let me slip away?" Hoag said. There was no pleading in his voice, only that old-man sound Carver hated.

"That would be a dumb idea," he said. "For all of us."

"No," Hoag said. "That would be the best thing. You know it would be."

"I'm not talking to you anymore," Carver shouted. "You can just shut up with that stuff because T.R. said you're going to stay put until we're gone, and that's how it is."

"You *know* what to do," Hoag said.

Carver expected Hoag to keep needling him, but the old man did shut up for many minutes, and when he spoke again it was to ask for his carving knife.

"With you having the gun," Hoag said, "what difference could it make?" He was turning the half-finished sculpture around in his hands.

Sure, Carver thought. But then he thought it wouldn't be so stupid to keep his hands busy. So Carver took the gun from his pants and held it against the chair back, then tossed the knife to the old man.

Hoag nodded. He opened the blade and flattened his big thumb alongside it and stared at the carving in his other hand. The features of the Indian's face had been roughed-in, the almond-shaped eyes already strong and sad-looking, and above them a headdress, a clump of fur and long buffalo horns with feathers and braids hanging down the neck.

Hoag pared into the wood gently. Carver watched, though his mind wandered. It was only after a few minutes that Carver realized that Hoag was bearing down deeper and deeper into the wood, cutting off one horn, then the other, then peeling the face away, strip by strip.

T.R. ordered Carver outside, shoving him toward the door with a sudden roughness. As he'd watched Hoag those last minutes, a trancelike calm had come over Carver, through which he heard the faint rhythmic wheezing of Hoag's breath and the slow slivering of the wood. He knew there was nothing more to say now, and it felt good. Then came the sharply whispered commands and T.R. bursting in to tie up the old man, a length of brand-new rope looped over his shoulder and neck, mountain-climber style. He looked all wrong.

Carver stood in the cold, rubbing his arm, already forgiving T.R. his edginess. Clare was with the horses. She'd found a man's peacoat and hugged it around herself, its shoulders drooping off her own. Carver walked past her and felt the bulging saddlebags.

"What's in there?" he said.

Clare shrugged. "Junk from the cabins," she said.

The split lip had not closed, and Carver watched her dabbing at it with her tongue.

"What he took don't make any sense," she said. "More guns." She turned away. "Nothing like what we need."

Carver figured she wanted to talk to him about as much as he did to her. Still, he wished they could get along. It would be easier over the border if there was trust between them. What lay ahead seemed suddenly enormous and foreign.

"Are you OK?" Carver asked quietly.

She stared back as if now he'd said something truly foolish.

"I'm sorry he had to hit you," Carver said, unsure what to add.

"There's nothing to say," Clare said.

Carver watched her walk away and stand by the car, watched her huddle on the back seat as if there were still security there. Carver stood with the horses, sliding his hand along the smooth slope of their necks, listening to the gentle grinding of their jaws against the bits, surrounded by their strong, reassuring smells.

There were no screams, no gunfire, only a silence that grew so deep that Carver, for all his natural inclination to stay put and wait, grew worried and finally broke from his spot and ran to the door of the trailer.

The knife was still in T.R.'s hand, the front of his shirt mushy with blood. Hoag was slumped on the couch, his head bent sharply against its arm. The slice in his neck had gone deep enough to cut both the artery and the windpipe. His face had drained to a grayish blue, the color of a winter dawn. Everything around Hoag was drenched. Carver had never seen so much blood, and the power with which it had left Hoag, splattering the wall clear to the ceiling, stopped him in his tracks.

T.R. turned on Carver. His breath was still deep from laboring with the bulk of the man's body. For the first time Carver read confusion in T.R.'s eyes and heard the slick, fast-talking mouth grope for words.

"You were going to tie him up," Carver said.

"He was a stupid old man," T.R. said.

"You weren't supposed to do that."

"All he had to do was sit still. It wasn't that goddamn complicated. All he had to do was what I told him."

Carver faced him. "I told him you were just going to tie him up until we were gone. That's what you said, and that's what I told him. Why'd you do this?"

"Richard," T.R. said. "This was an accident here."

Carver could not help staring at the body, awful as it was, so hulking and freshly dead.

"It wasn't no accident, T.R."

"I'm telling you what it was," T.R. said. "It just happened. It wasn't nobody's fault but his."

Carver knew as surely as he knew anything that this was a lie and that he was as close to the heart of it as if he'd held the knife in his own hand. His stomach clenched. "T.R. . . ," he said, his voice reduced to a gauzy whisper, rays of metallic energy flooding his limbs.

T.R. shook him hard. "You listen now, you go and get her in here and we'll clean this up." And when Carver didn't move, he pushed past him and ran out to bring his wife back, leaving Carver alone again with Hoag. It was perfectly quiet then as Carver stood inert, looking at Hoag with eyes as wooden as any staring down from the paneled walls. The noise of strong voices had finally abandoned him, left him reeling in the terrible emptiness of his own thoughts.

These things Carver remembered distinctly, though most of what came afterward was a blur through which he saw T.R.'s true colors, which weren't colors at all down deep, he finally understood, but only a brittle glaze on top. For a few minutes they tried to straighten things up in the trailer, T.R. pretending they could make it look like they'd never been there, finally placing the knife in Hoag's hand and rolling him over and ordering them into the car, at the last slapping the horses loose into the frozen fields, still with their saddles on.

At the end of the Mullan's Crossing Road they turned, but away from Canada. T.R. drove now, with Clare beside him and Carver crouched in back, watching the dawn begin. By the time they reached pavement, logging trucks were barreling down the center of the road. T.R. swerved again and again, the wheel responding sluggishly to his jerky movements. Carver understood it was all out of his hands now.

The first border they crossed was into Idaho, not to a new life but to a gun battle with state police—which T.R. might have avoided had he not stupidly tried to sell some of the guns in a bar along the highway. Over the sound of shots and T.R.'s shouting, Clare had begun to laugh, a shrill baying that left Carver on the floor of the car, his hands over his ears.

He could still see Hoag's big body on the couch and wondered what it was that the man had wanted to tell him. It didn't matter, of course. He would imagine Hoag many times during the months it took to get the three of them back across the border into Montana, and through the trial and the hysteria T.R. aroused in the packed courtroom, and as he read the version of himself in the daily paper, and even later as he sat handcuffed in the light plane, the clean late sunlight falling on the blue vein of the North Fork outside the little window.

Hardest of all was to imagine Hoag standing up from the couch and shuffling past him to the door, squeezing him on the shoulder like a friendly old grandfather and saying, "You done right this time, boy." Hoag would walk down the drive, turn at the road, and hobble through moonlight to the dark edge of the trees and disappear. Carver never knew what he would have told T.R., but he knew that with a little effort he could have thought of something.

Saving Graces

"Jesus God," LaDonna says. "Here comes The Wild Bunch."

Earl half-slumps in his wooden wheelchair, snow like fallen pin-feathers on his sloping shoulders, big hands dormant in his lap. Propelling him into the Antlers Bar strides Iron Eyes, estranged full-blood Crow, Earl's Number One, a stalwart larch post of a man.

"Clear the track!" says Iron Eyes, though there is no one anywhere near being in the way. Except for a couple of solitaries at the bar and one spindly cowboy arguing with the pay phone, the place is deserted. Thirty-eight pairs of dusty antlers tangle in perfect silence on the side wall. Some nights a card game flourishes in back, but this being Tuesday, and with the snow, the dealer showed up earlier, sat yawning awhile under a shaft of yellowish light, then went home without so much as breaking the seal off the first deck.

Earl tilts his face to the lights and hollers, a grating, directionless sort of holler. When it has died away, he returns his face to the deep shadows of his hat brim. Iron Eyes guides them to their table, turns to regard the door: in scoots Sugar Baby.

"Just like a hummingbird," Iron Eyes says. "Always moving, never keep up."

Earl nods with his whole upper body, more a restive lurch than an agreement.

Sugar Baby hovers up to the table, lips aflutter.

"Hey, hey," Sugar Baby squeals. "Gonna have some kind of good time."

LaDonna's eyes drop shut like two dusty Venetian blinds. Meadowlarks were abundant in her girlhood. Crushing the edge of her bed, her father sang his only daughter to sleep, slow rhyming songs that merged with the growing darkness. Mornings, her smile floated in the oval mirror of the dressing table, patient, secure; her hair tumbled naturally to her shoulders. So why now, she wonders, do twelve inches of silver-blue swirl rise from her forehead like a lacquered canary cage? Why does she fix drinks for drunks? What kind of ambition is that?

Across the bar, fiddling with the loose change in a black plastic ashtray, stands Betsy Bell, a muffin-faced high-school graduate. This is her first night on the job and her calves hurt. For the past hour she's been saying things like, "Now you'd think I never stood up a day in my life . . ." and now she says, "What's *that?*"

"Just please don't ask me," LaDonna says.

"What's The Wild Bunch?"

"You think *you* got a pain."

Ignoring the glossy half-moons painted on the lids, LaDonna kneads her eyes, and she can see colors no one else can see: Northern Lights. Monarch butterflies twisting airborne from the sleepy milkweed of the borrow pits.

Sugar Baby has dropped four dollars' worth of sweaty quarters into the jukebox and now squats before the speaker grille, brandishing his red, white, and blue, Japanese-made, cassette tape recorder. It goes everywhere with him—hangs on a hook in the barn as he sweeps, hours on end, hangs from the handlebars of his bicycle, keeping the air around him always busy with sound. Tonight he's chosen Freddy Fender, has punched every song of his the jukebox holds, multiple times, and grins up at the others with the feverish grin of a forty-two-year-old child.

I'll be there, Freddy Fender sings, *before the next teardrop falls.*

The voice is oily, whiskey-colored. Any place but this, in daylight, it would not be tolerated. But here it seems to rise up agreeably from the collective mush of broken pacts and forgiveness.

"I got tears you can't even see," LaDonna says.

"Huh?"

"Nothing," LaDonna says. "Here, the Rainier goes to the Indian. Earl, he's the one in the chair, he gets the two Southern Comforts."

"What about him?" Betsy Bell asks, nodding toward Sugar Baby.

"He don't drink," LaDonna says. "Thank Christ."

LaDonna watches Betsy Bell serve. *Pert,* she thinks, *deliver me from pert.* Betsy Bell is the third new bar girl she's had to break in in the last six months. Where do these nitwits come from, she wonders, though it's no mystery.

Wasted days, Freddy Fender sings. *Wasted nights.*

Thinking tonight's variation on *God, have I seen this all,* she bends, the turkey skin of her elbows adhering lightly to the varnished bar. She watches Earl, and Earl, who surely feels her attention, doesn't look up.

Crippled in ways that show and don't show, Earl is nonetheless the unchallenged leader of this bunch. Father of strays, some have called him. A soft touch. It is true that a number of marginal types have come and gone from Earl's ranch over the years—though mostly they have stayed and done the work with an odd dedication. Kinder souls in town have seen more than softheadedness in Earl's way of managing things. Now in middle-age, he is the surviving son of a man who laid his hand on a thousand-some acres of timber and dark-soiled bottomland, back in a time when desire alone could make it so. By now there are few who remember with any accuracy that father, his narrow little eyes, his high ambition, the ways he drained alternatives from those close by him. They say the one has to pass on before the next can come to fruit. They say there are all kinds of accidents, accidents of birth among them. There's no telling what Earl might have turned into otherwise.

How much do you save out of a life, LaDonna wonders.

She can remember the ranch in its prime: the main house standing white and manorly in the shade of tall-grown cottonwood, a herd of Appaloosa sprinting in clear midday sunlight, cattle feeding in significant numbers off toward the swell of foothills. Remembers it as if it would always be like it was.

She watches his big hands folded before him on the table, the two shots still untouched, imagines his slow switchbacks into memory. She turns her back on all of it, pours herself a few fingers of Wild Turkey, and touches the glass to the geranium glaze of her lips.

One night years ago, a hard freeze on the fields, Earl and LaDonna came into the light and noise of the Antlers, carried along by separate groups of friends: Earl in his mid-twenties then, broad-smiling, and gently flamboyant, LaDonna somewhat underaged but tall and sassy-enough looking so it hardly mattered.

One slow song she found herself with Earl and tucked her face into the hollow of his neck and let herself be surrounded by his fragrant slow-spinning presence. Later they had gone out into the night, boozy and nuzzling, Earl warbling into the haze of chimney smoke and far-off lights, now and then backing LaDonna against a parked car, LaDonna saying, "Hey, now . . ." and laughing uncautiously. And when he kissed her, LaDonna kissed him back, her hands up under his jacket, feeling the hard pattern of muscle, and she understood that this was a grown-up and looked at him with surprise when he circled her back to the Antlers for a last round of dancing when, maybe, she would have followed him anywhere. And when she got home that night she undressed, steadying herself with the bedpost, and slid naked between flannel sheets, thinking there was something altogether different about this man Earl, and it was more than the refinements of age, and by the time her imagining dispersed into sleep she was happy for herself in one of the oldest and simplest ways.

The year's first snow was falling in the morning as she sat around her parents' house shrugging off twinges of embarrassment. You were a fool if you put much stock in what went on late at night. Above all, she was patient, in no particular hurry. Her friend Cassie had left town graduation summer, saying she wanted a life with some kind of *style* to it, if LaDonna knew what she meant, and LaDonna got letters from San Diego and Laguna Beach and read them carefully and wasn't tempted. Her other friend of long standing was Patsy Anderson—now Patsy Slovik—who was already spinning for the second time in the great pastel vortex of baby showers, which was OK, LaDonna thought, if that was what you wanted. LaDonna didn't spend much time putting a face on the future. She knew only that it was there, and she would walk out to meet it and it would take care of her.

Her parents were still at church and the fumes from the pork roast in the oven had driven her onto the porch, where she sat in a brittle wicker lawn chair watching the snow come down. And then she saw Earl's two-tone pickup pull up the driveway and saw him get out and approach her, amiable, breaking tradition. LaDonna could see no reason to camouflage her amazement.

"Damn," she grinned, thinking: *Earl, you look good to me, you really do.*

Earl stood at the bottom of the porch steps, smiling, too, but with a glaze of seriousness.

"I woke up," he said, "and I saw you riding a horse."

He shuffled, checked the sky.

"Can you ride?"

"Yeah," LaDonna said. "I can ride."

She went inside and scribbled a note for her parents and left it on the front table, hopped into Earl's pickup, and slid over near him on the seat. She remembers how it felt: that being just on the edge of a thing, all of it lying there before her like a field without tracks, the urge to go momentarily balanced by the urge to hang back and look and savor it.

Earl drove them back to the ranch, and they saddled the horses and rode out along the slow curves of the Shields River, LaDonna handling the horse easily, though for a town girl riding was a thing out of childhood, Earl beside her, strong but somehow ungainly in the saddle. They stopped later and built a fire of driftwood sticks and sat near each other on the rocks, watching the last ducks of the season materialize out of the snowy sky and skid down to the black, slow-running water.

"You're a funny one," she told Earl that day.

Earl shook his head, smiling still.

"Here I thought nothing was going to come of you," she said. "Thought you were going to be just one night."

"You just never know," Earl said, his eyes fixed on the rising braid of smoke.

He took her hand with a shy delicacy, as if they hadn't pressed full-length against each other the night before, as if attractions and histories didn't accumulate, as if things happened only once.

Earl disappeared into ranch work for a week and didn't call, though LaDonna hardly expected him to. The season struggled beteen the final strength of Indian summer and the true descent of winter. Saturday night LaDonna stayed in and kept her mother company, at the last minute afraid she might run into him out in the crowd, maybe not alone. But Sunday he came again to get her—as if there'd been an arrangement—and they rode all afternoon along the ragged boundaries of Earl's father's land, Earl beginning to come out of himself, pointing with a kind of pride at what lay in front of them, far and vivid in the broken sunlight.

Snow was coming out of the northwest when Earl appeared the next Sunday. LaDonna sang lightly to the radio as she watched the fenceposts smear past beyond the borrow pits, now and then glancing at Earl who seemed quieter than normal. Twice she tried to draw him into talk, but he gave her a refractory smile and said, "It's nothing," which hardly satisfied her. Like the first day, they rode along the river bank, though now the ground was cold enough to hold snow. Earl let his horse walk most of the time, and LaDonna walked hers, an arm's length away. They passed slowly by the scattered leavings of their fire but didn't stop. She took a hard look at Earl, wondering if he was happy enough with the way things stood, wondering if maybe she'd gotten too close and somehow scared him, made him stop and consider exactly what it was he wanted from her.

"Getting late," LaDonna said finally.

She swung around and dug her heels in and took off, cantering across the empty pasture, lifting high out of the saddle, blinking into the rush of cold air, breaking then into a full gallop. She could feel Earl come up alongside and match her acceleration, and she kept her eyes on the near-distance where the Crazy Mountains loomed green-black and stark. She knew precisely where he was. Then she turned, her hair whirling a crosscurrent in her face, and he was not there beside her, and turning farther back she saw Earl's mare grinding head-down in the frozen grass. Earl forward on the bent neck, stunned in the stirrups, and, as LaDonna reined around, the horse rolled full-over, its front leg shattered below the knee and dangling, and she saw Earl disappear under the weight and when she saw him again he was perfectly still, face down in a ring of strewn snow.

LaDonna jumped down and turned Earl's face to the light and wiped the snow and blood from his eyes. Close by, the horse was thrashing the ground in a squall of terrible screaming. It tried to muscle back to its feet and collapsed again, the back legs kicking random jabs into the air.

"Get up!" she yelled at Earl, almost a reflex since she knew already he could no more get up than fly away. She took his wrists and dragged him out of range and slipped off her jacket and laid it over him, though it barely covered his chest, before thinking maybe she shouldn't have done that, moved him, maybe you weren't supposed to do that, knowing, too, there was no choice about it.

She knelt and rubbed his face and sensed that he was conscious and understood.

"I've got to leave you," she said. "I don't want to."

She followed the river back through the trail of paired tracks, almost buried with snow, the burn of helplessness overwhelming as she aimed for the main house and people little better than strangers with names, who would not be able to avoid hating her for the rest of their lives, when otherwise they might have taken her in as family and watched over the flowering of her children.

They took Earl out of the field in the bed of a pickup, into the house and into town and later to the hospital in Bozeman, where he stayed for weeks, the nerves in his spine crushed, as the doctors and everyone else waited to see how much of him could be salvaged.

On the third day LaDonna borrowed her mother's wood-paneled station wagon and set out alone for the hospital and got to Livingston and stopped to try and find something to take with her to give him, and then, adrift in the middle of the drugstore, realized—though she couldn't explain it—that she was going to have to turn around and go home. Her mother said it was only right to go and see the man, and LaDonna remembers so clearly standing in that long-gone kitchen saying, "I know. I know."

But she didn't go and the longer she stayed away, the more she understood there was nothing to say, and then the staying away itself became a reason. Considering it carefully, she understood that her connection was to something that happened, something that came once and moved on, leaving her by herself, free-standing. It was not to the man—she barely knew him.

So she never did go to him.

When she thought of him, at first, the memory was raw, a growing thing just pried from the soil, now left root-bare in a harsh light. But later, hearing of his ranch, noticing his name time and again in the newspaper—so many head sold at livestock auction—hearing of his mother's death, then a year later, his father's, she found the memory had overgrown with kinder sensations; they had only missed each other, as people sometimes do.

The summer after Earl's fall she started going out with the son of the local Ford dealer and surprised herself a year later by marrying him—surprised herself most because until that time she'd never been aware of doing a thing simply because it would make her feel normal and unobtrusive. She knew within weeks it was a mistake and that was another new feeling, that sense of having veered away, and she didn't even know from what.

She thinks of her twenties and what chills her most is that they are complete and sealed, more finished even than her thirties, which have disappeared like water vapor. She thinks of a time of excuses and of staying up all night listening to a whiney husband, of crying alone over egg-crusted breakfast dishes, knowing even then it was a kind of training. So when, in the seventh year of revolving pain and numbness, the man packed off to Spokane with the dealership's clerk/typist (a woman she had once heard her husband describe as *really something),* LaDonna was angry—at him for being so perfectly predictable, and at herself for knowing that she understood it all and still went ahead and wasted so many good nights playing out the loss. But underneath the anger was relief and it was genuine, and she found that being by herself had its compensations. For the better part of a year she cashed his alimony checks, unhappily, and when the man defaulted it seemed like nothing more than the butt end of a bad thing. So another spring night, a lifetime ago, she fixed herself up and returned to the Antlers and started serving.

When did I change, LaDonna wonders, *when did I get like this?*

The jukebox has silenced itself, and Sugar Baby has hastily rewound the cassette, and the Antlers is awash with tinselly ballads, Freddy Fender singing through a length of irrigation pipe.

"Some kind of fancy crooner, no?" says Sugar Baby.

Iron Eyes frowns solemnly.

"Want to break your little heart," Sugar Baby goes on.

Earl suddenly shudders from the waist up, as if sloughing off a skim of ice.

"Shut it down," he says. "Christ, boy, there's limits. . . ."

Iron Eyes cracks a thin, sympathetic smile, shakes his head. "He can't let nothing go."

Sugar Baby kills the music. Earl pumps back the two shots, leans forward with his arms flat to the table, and lets the burn take immediate possession of his insides.

"Don't know why I put up with you," Earl says.

"You need me," Sugar Baby replies with full certainty.

"Like a man needs a good lesson," Earl says.

He looks up into the glow of LaDonna's attention, then evades it.

Sugar Baby is ready to banter, but Earl doesn't speak and when he does finally it is to Iron Eyes.

"OK, Chief," he says. "Time to make a trip."

The Indian stands and wheels Earl toward the hall to the men's room, and they are followed, shortly, by the Sugar Baby.

Betsy Bell is shifting the weight of responsibility from one foot to the other.

"They're *weird. . . ,*" she says.

"You think so?" LaDonna says.

"They give me the creeps. How come they come in here?"

What would you do, where would you go? LaDonna wants to say, but she keeps her mouth shut this once. There is a world of things she doesn't say. There are gaps and she is tired. She fills Betsy Bell's tray with another round.

"Do you know they got to stand him up in there to piss?" LaDonna says in a minute.

"I never thought about that."

"No," says LaDonna, pouring now into her own glass. "I didn't figure you had."

Betsy Bell gives her a funny look.

"Something the matter?" LaDonna inquires, lowering her sooty lashes at the girl.

"I didn't think bartenders drank. That's what I always heard. No offense or nothing."

"Now I'm going to tell you something for your own good," LaDonna says. "I wouldn't be twenty again for anything in this world."

She drinks and abandons the glass on the drainboard, then walks away from Betsy Bell and goes to the door and outside and stands on the boardwalk where the snow has eased a little, too late to matter. The street looks untraveled, insulated against loud noise. Her exhaled breath hangs for a moment in the still air. Hugging her bare arms, LaDonna looks across the street at the dark face of the Mercantile, out of business for years, and reads the big banner still plastered to the front window: EVERYTHING MUST GO.

LaDonna hides in the shadow of the doorway, ready to go back, and is caught up short by the wall of buck heads, as if she had never really seen them before. They look so little noble she wants to cry, so stiff with dust and inattention it seems impossible to believe their power and grace ever caused a man to hesitate behind his trigger. And she realizes that as long as she has been here there have never been any new ones, though every year the animals still die up the draws, crashing through crusted snow as if their uplifted racks were suddenly too much to support. And the people below, bunched together in the circle of electric light, seem too small, so many cripples, and it strikes LaDonna just then that despite everything, that is one thing she is not.

Earl has emptied his glasses again and is pestering Betsy Bell with drunken curses, and she's gotten skittery and is holding her distance.

"Don't you be that way," LaDonna tells him. "There's no need."

She snatches the tray out of Betsy Bell's hands and circles the bar and loads it with bottles and carries it out front to the table and sits down.

"What am I supposed to do?" Betsy Bell asks.

"Do what you want," LaDonna says. "Go home to your husband."

LaDonna draws Earl into her sights.

"Take off your hat, Earl."

"What?"

"So I can see what you've turned yourself into."

"Take off that hat, Daddy," echoes Sugar Baby.

LaDonna stretches across the table and lifts the hat with both hands and gives it over to Iron Eyes, who holds it like some sacred artifact. Matted strands of grayish hair cling to Earl's head. It looks exposed and vulnerable.

"Worse than I imagined," LaDonna says.

Earl shrugs, flicks his eyes away, but can't help turning back to her.

"What was it you were looking for?" he says.

"Now you got me there," she says.

She makes a move to refill the glasses, but Earl lays a hand over the top of his.

"Just looking, I guess," LaDonna says. "Curious."

"It don't pay."

"I don't know, Earl. I don't know about you. I think you turned slow and foolish. What do you think about that?"

"I say I think it don't pay."

"Think you're beyond hope?" LaDonna says. "Out of range?"

She tips back in her chair for the long view: Earl, flanked as always by Iron Eyes and the benign little Sugar Baby. She sees how he resides in their center, how hulking and bruised and paternal he is.

"I'll tell you what I think," she says. "I think it's getting late in this place, Earl."

There are tears in the rims of Earl's eyes as he stares across this distance at LaDonna, and when he finally blinks they glint on his cheeks like starlight.

LaDonna sweeps down on him.

"Don't you do that. Not here."

She wipes his lids with her long curved thumbs. She turns aside to Betsy Bell, who is hovering like a lost handmaiden.

"Goddamn it," she yells. "You go and play some real music. You hear?"

Betsy Bell startles from her daze and goes and begins punching life into the jukebox.

"And turn it up."

In a moment the tunes blare out from all corners of the room, a swarm of guitars and tenor horns and human voices.

LaDonna turns back to the man.

"Now you get up," she says.

Earl looks brutalized: she has no right.

"Can't do!" shrieks Sugar Baby. "Can't do!"

"Get up! You're going to dance with me," LaDonna says. "I know, it don't make any difference."

She stands abruptly and begins to pull the table away from between them.

"Come on now," she says to The Wild Bunch. "Get him up."

She plunges her hands under his arms and buries her face in the opening of his coat and tugs against him. Iron Eyes rises and takes Earl's arm and lifts him from the chair as he has done a thousand times, but with a new motive now, which he seems to understand and conspire to, and Sugar Baby pops to his feet and lets the other heavy arm encircle his skinny shoulders.

They lurch into the empty dance floor, the four of them, clinging and staggering, Earl's boots dragging along on the gritty hardwood, LaDonna humming, her cheek upturned to the blue light. And then, as if things happened for a good reason, the music composes itself around them, slows to the tempo of the human heart when it pounds in answer to the real work of pleasure and survival, and—Betsy Bell looking on in wonder—they spin together for a moment in a graceful knot.

Other People's Stories

The late afternoon sun catches her suitcase where it lies shut on my bed. Pools of light dance at its brass latches. Outside, a thick granular haze hangs over the bay. The shoreline shimmers passively, the waves collect impressions of an empty sky. No one out there is in a hurry.

"Where will you go?" I ask her.

She stares into the slow-running drain of the bathroom sink. Her tanned legs are magnificent against the tiny white tiles. I watch the cool, curving skin of the ankles, the strap of the sandal, the gentle filigree that hangs along her thighs. My attraction seems undiluted by all the time that has come between us. I'm ready to live my life again.

She seems lost in thought, watching the water curl out of sight. In even the fastest-running of us there are sometimes eddies, returns. If I were younger I might think she is posing or stalling—but there is no explaining to be done now. I know my rights: they are momentary and, like the waves, don't accumulate. It doesn't matter how she has managed to track me down to this backwater kitchenette, or what kind of artifact she has made of these fifteen years. If she has suffered, the scars are hidden. She's as untempered as ever. All day I've denied myself the one question that matters—why has she come?—for fear of dispersing this strange satisfaction that surrounds me. I feel as blue and hushed as the horizon.

It was that same suitcase she took south to Phoenix with her that night, except it was not filled with these light durable clothes then, the wardrobe of an habitual traveler. It was stuffed with her work, her designs on the lay of the land. Hundreds of sketches in fine brown ink: rows of bristling evergreens, expanses of clipped lawn, geometric gardens, terraced pools with fountains whose water sprayed high into the air and never fell.

All into the bag, all gone. I never thought I'd see the least bit of it again.

In the spring of 1964 I was thirty-two, living alone in a peaceable, though largely unexamined, happiness, purged of any earlier expectations about where my life was headed. I'd begun my career writing for a daily paper, but found my disposition at odds with its pace, with its disinterested point of view. I tried some free-lancing, got a break, and then another, eventually developing into a better-than-average hack with as much work as I needed to keep the rent paid and my mind occupied. By that spring my name had appeared many times in print, prefaced by *As Told To,* nearly invisible beside names that came readily to people's tongues. That was the way I wanted it.

I brought a promise: in my care, a lifetime's entanglements, intrigues, sundry insights, and bafflements would make a story strangers could believe. Vaudevillians and torch-singers came to me with their secret lives. Mothers of famous sons and daughters confided in me; widows wept openly. Survivors of crashes and kidnappings let me recreate their abandonment and their hope. I learned to be patient with the silences, the fractured moods. I didn't judge, I didn't tell them they were lying or too ordinary for fame. Who was I to say? It was an honor to hear their stories. I did my best to remain a ghost behind them.

I'd been working on a magazine piece, a *Where Are They Now?* about some stars of the silent movies. Earlier that week I'd recorded the venomous recollections of an aging swashbuckler turned political commentator and visited a slapstick artist in the sunroom of his nursing home. Friday I drove up to meet Amy Neihardt, the child-bride in *The Harvest,* the beautiful, mischievous angel in *Faraday's Dream.* She had the kind of huge, round eyes that give a young woman the illusion of great age yet, when she has become old, make her seem nearly girlish. I knew she had been out of the movies since 1927, but I didn't know why and I was unprepared for her candor.

She sat across from me, tiny, wild-haired, directing her unsparing reminiscences at my Wollensak, every few minutes leaning forward and plucking a Pall Mall from a wooden box (the sound of its lid knocking like a slow metronome in the background of the tape). She had married her director and, surrendering to his jealousy, had agreed to live in the drafty villa he bought for her and to make no more films. She had a child and later divorced the director, but he had power among the studios and convinced everyone she was too unstable to work. She remarried and went abroad for several years, hoping the time away would allow her a fresh start, but this husband suffered an alcoholic breakdown in Venice, and on the return voyage he disappeared overboard one night. Madness followed her daughter as well. A gentle child, she had grown distant at puberty, then swiftly catatonic enough to be institutionalized. It went on, a litany of misfortune that should have left her bitter or religious; yet what emerged was a portrait of bewilderment and endurance.

I tell myself these things happen, she said on the tape. *I don't feel sorry for myself, but sometimes it seems hard to believe all of this has been my life. I wonder if I didn't get confused with some of the parts I had. I don't remember why I did some of the things I did. Sometimes I think I was just washed along with the current, and sometimes I feel terribly responsible. Who knows?*

She stopped and smiled at me, though only half her face responded, as though numbed with Novocain.

Maybe it's just foolhardy to try and track it all down, she said after a minute, looked at me and then down at the old movie stills I'd brought with me.

"Put those away, would you?" she said.

There was a soft knock on the door, and a younger woman entered with an armful of papers. She was lovely, willowy, and finely dressed, with thick cinnamon hair fanning her shoulders. Miss Neihardt introduced us.

"Molly," she said. "Mr. Hanna is going to tell everyone what's become of me. I trust he will be . . . respectful."

Molly eyed me with arched brows. She had a cool direct gaze that caught me up short. I felt like an intruder. I packed my things and thanked Miss Neihardt and headed for the door. I hesitated as I reached it, turned, and caught Molly gunning a bright smile at me.

Outside, the fog was burning off the valley. I started my old Ford, checked my watch, and decided I'd have enough time to hear the whole tape before an afternoon meeting. But I killed the engine and sat in the car, unwilling to move. I watched the front door of the house in my rear-view. I got out and paced the drive, ending up at her little car, a red MG with its top down. I pictured her at its wheel, those long legs sliding down to the pedals, flying north on the coast highway, ninety miles an hour against the glaring Pacific sun. I hopped over the door, slipped down into the passenger seat, and waited.

"Well," she said, dropping her folders behind the seat, "what an interesting development."

Our first weekend boiled down to the fact we didn't know each other, a privileged time we'd have only once. I had borrowed a friend's cabin in the foothills. She told me she had work to finish and insisted on driving herself, so I left her an elaborate map and went up early, needling and second-guessing myself all the way. I had fires going in the cookstove and the fireplace and was sitting on the porch steps watching the sky fade, nearly convinced she wouldn't come, when her headlights cut through the trees and shone in my eyes.

"You found me," I said.

"Were you hiding?" she answered, unslinging the bag from her shoulder.

Not at all, I thought. I wanted her terribly. We ate and collapsed on my friend's overstuffed sofa and talked most of the night, taking feverish digressions through our histories, staking greater and greater claims on each other. I couldn't take my eyes off her as she got up, now and then, to replenish her tea. She moved with a limber, tomboy's grace, the shadows playing down the ribs in her leotard. Her voice was a soft staccato: her mouth flickered into a host of smiles, each of which was a new mood for me to follow.

When we woke, the window shone with a milky light. In the distance I heard the whine of logging trucks downshifting at the grade, and closer, the sharp calls of magpies from the low branches of the aspen. The air was cool, scented with a trace of tamarack smoke. I wanted not to move, not to set time rolling again. Then the moment was broken by the weight of her hands on my shoulders. *I want you,* she said. *Yes,* I answered, *I want you, too.* Did she know I'd never said that to a woman before? She held me, directed me. Her body was urgent, confident of its power and sleekness. We laughed and floated and cried out in the sheer pleasure of being so close, so responsible for each other's flight and return. We slept again. When I woke for the second time, she was up and dressed, winding film in her camera with sharp flicks of the wrist.

"Good," she said. "I thought maybe I'd put you in a coma."

By the afternoon we were tangled under the comforter again, less and less strangers, and that night, laughing and trying to catch her breath, she said, "Hanna, you better watch out or you'll be writing about us."

In the rush of good feeling that flooded me those next weeks, there was a trace of something sour, a harsh whisper telling me I'd wasted too much of my life. Though she was only a few years younger, she seemed to come from another, more exuberant, self-directed generation. The joy of abandoning myself to her—which I did gladly—was not quite enough to wipe away the knowledge that things had been pretty dull before her. It was as if I'd never allowed myself any genuine excitement. She made me see how compulsive I'd been, how little I questioned my routine. I met expectations, made deadlines, honored contracts; and was satisfied, true, but never exhilarated. Now I had a choice: regret the man I'd been, or turn my back on him and run ahead with her.

The spring rains broke overnight, and the sky was deep and lovely the day she moved in. I'd lived by myself in that overlarge upstairs floor of rooms, without so much as a parakeet for company, since the year Eisenhower beat Stevenson for the last time. It delighted me to have her there. Her plants filled the windows, her fragrance lingered in the air. The two rooms she chose to work in came alive. They'd been dead space before her, a place to pace and stare down desultorily at the neighbor's trash cans when my concentration failed. She assaulted them with her presence. The walls became a pastiche of illustrations, pages delicately razored from glossy magazines, blueprints, street maps from around the country, blow-ups of ornamental shrubs and trees (blue spruce, dogwood, nine-bark bursting with tiny white blossoms), and sheets of drawing paper full of questions written in her tall, precise lettering, each of which she would eventually consider and dispose of with a neat horizontal line.

She hovered over her work in a controlled frenzy. Possibilities floated across her imagination like an endless succession of fair weather clouds drifting into shapes. Her hand skated over the page; the lines were light, yet exact, as if etched in crystal. She flipped pages briskly, beginning again, pausing with a slight squint, changing the angle on what she'd already done, or the scale, or the mood. I had to sequester myself in order to work and even then distractions beckoned me like a gang of urchins; but she didn't mind my frequent intrusions, my foolish questions. She could talk without interrupting the communion between hand and eye. Finally her landscape would fall into alignment. She'd tuck the pen behind her ear and smile up richly, suddenly including me in the wild precision of her gaze.

I soon changed my mind about the magazine piece, in favor of doing a longer profile of Amy Neihardt. I was touched by the way she took her losses—was it grace or fatalism? Molly had known her for several years—they'd served on a committee for the city once—but she'd never seen any of her pictures. "She doesn't have copies," Molly told me. "They were all made by her first husband, and she won't give him the satisfaction. Even dead." I discovered that there were long sequences from several of them included in *Silent Film, Volume 4,* which our museum owned. Molly and I watched them one night in July. On the way home she was unusually quiet. I asked her what she thought.

"It's awful to see her so young," Molly said. "Before any of it happened. She looked so confident. That must be the real reason she won't look at them. It would make you always go back trying to figure out the exact place it all went wrong."

"She had some bad luck," I said.

"Possibly. But luck doesn't explain anything; it's just there, like one of the elements."

She took my arm. "Hanna," she said. "Do you have to write about her?"

"I was hoping you'd help me."

"I'd rather not," she said.

The next afternoon I was replaying the tape with the door slightly ajar when I heard the phone ring. As Miss Neihardt spoke, I heard Molly answer it in the background. For a few moments the voices of the two women played simultaneously in my ears: Miss Neihardt's raspy as a gust of dried leaves; Molly's smooth and muscular, arranging her client's thoughts for him.

She stuck her head in and said she was going out. She disappeared with pad and camera until much later, when I was in the kitchen fussing with our dinner. I'd always cooked respectable meals for myself—the alternative being too symptomatic of my life in general, tacos in greasy paper, cole slaw from a plastic container—so I continued. Molly liked what I made, but otherwise she didn't take much interest in food. She had never bothered to learn how to cook and would go for days, I was sure, on nothing more substantial than Ry-Krisp and tea with honey.

I shoved the manicotti in the oven and went to visit her in the darkroom (formerly a walk-in closet under the eaves). I watched her slip the blowups from tray to tray. She kept working as I put my arms around her waist. One by one the prints emerged from the last bath and were hung to dry. Shots of backyards, entranceways, courtyards, corridors of that odd no-man's-land around office buildings.

I nuzzled at her neck, but a light tilt of the head told me to wait.

"There's no people," I said, looking over her shoulder.

"No," she said. "But there will be."

She held up an eight-by-ten. "See, look, they'll come out and sit in the sun and eat their lunches and talk to their friends."

She pointed to the spots where the benches would be. I could picture her moving the people around with the ease I'd once moved toy animals around my train set.

"Don't be long," I said.

She gave my hand a quick kiss, then turned back to the enlarger. "Just a few more," she said. But the time got away from her, and later I put tinfoil on the dinner and put it in the refrigerator.

As the summer wore on, I was certain I was living the best time of my life, more consecutive good days than I'd ever thought was possible. My work absorbed me. The choices came easily, as if from a subconscious harmony. The words clicked off the typewriter as fast as I could imagine them. Whatever I did, she was there in my thoughts, a bright chunk of future, a bonus I never could have predicted.

One night we were lying in bed listening to a slow sax tune drift in from the other room. We had made love and rested and come awake again. She was curled against me, hands spread along my ribs, her face aimed away toward the open window. She talked about us, about our love as if it were something outside us, an artifact we had made with our desire.

"Don't let anything happen to it," she said.

"No," I said.

"Nothing's ever been like this. I never knew there was a man like you," she said, almost solemnly. "Do you love me wildly?"

"Of course."

"Beyond reason?"

I drew her tighter to me and let her fragrance lift me into her earnest vision of us, praying nothing would come to make me desert it. Part of me was embarrassed at her extravagance—how could I be that special? The rest of me was overcome—by naiveté and gratitude and love. As I held her, her breath slowed and she settled into a heavy sleep, though I stayed awake for a long time.

We were driving one day in early October. The weather had held and the year seemed poised exactly between seasons. We rose and fell through the foothills, the air a frantic rush in our ears. I had nothing special on my mind, except how much I liked watching her maneuver that car—so much a part of her: the sureness of the gear-shifting, her shoulders leaning into the curves, the wild tasseling of her hair.

Eventually the light and buoyancy of the day gave out, and we returned to the city. Driving one-handed, she wiggled into her jacket, aiming her fine chin at the sunset. We cut past the unplanted, newly paved subdivisions where the houses sat like single scoops of sherbet, past the mobile-home parks into the scruffier fringes of the city, tall frame houses, their tin roofs flashing the sun in our eyes. There were jacks under the corners of porches, siding dappled with primer, tarpaper battened with lath, tricycles and realty signs and dog burrowings in the yards, now and then a tangle of begonias or a few pots of crusty geraniums, some lawn chairs, an old woman on hands and knees, weeding and shouting at a miniature terrier.

I turned to smile at her—*isn't life a gas*—but she met me with an unfamiliar look: disgust, impatience? Was it aimed at me? I felt at home on streets like those, not so different from my neighborhood where I could walk after dinner on sidewalks buckled open by elms long-dead and sawed down, stepping on the paw-tracks of cats who lived in my father's time.

"Jesus," she said. "This certainly has gotten tacky over here."

I let it pass. Earlier I'd asked her to show me her first piece of work for the city, a park across town. She agreed, reluctantly, so we kept going, right-angled our way northeast, across the river and the tracks.

She ground the tires in the gravel and killed the engine, jumped out leaving the door agape. The park was below us, a bowl-shaped two or three acres. The grass looked abused, hard as a schoolyard. Along the far edge lay an open trench with sections of concrete pipe dumped here and there in the dirt. We made our way down to the center, where there was a disk of turgid water and a cluster of cement things. I must have looked bewildered.

"They're lambs, for God's sake."

There was no point in quibbling. They looked bad enough as it was, anointed with worms of spray paint and smudged with god-knows-what. She stood among them, hands on hips, frowning. Suppertime had emptied the park of dogwalkers and football tossers. The wind stirred the papery leaves at our feet.

"This is such crap," she said.

"I know," I said. "But listen, what can you do? After you make it, it's out of your hands."

She shook her head. "Do you see why I don't come back to these places?" She sat astride the back of one of her lambs, squeezing the life out of its neck.

"Sometimes I feel like there's waves following me," she said, no longer at me, but studying the slow approach of a man in an oily peacoat.

"Wiping it all out," she said. "Making it crazy."

He was a boy really, clutching a paper sack to his chest, coming down toward us as if on a mission. His eyes were as black as his coat and seemed to float in their sockets at odd angles. I thought I'd seen him before, downtown on the streets near the station or stopped halfway across one of our bridges, watching the river flash beneath him as if it were a reflection of his thoughts.

He stood over her, soaking up her horror. He went to the mouth of the bag with one hand. She flinched; I got ready to move. But I could see that inside the bag there was only a busted pillow case.

He waved his hand through the air, sprinkling feathers behind it. They settled softly on her hair and shoulders.

"Pixie dust," he said.

He came to me next and dipped into the bag again and let his silly benevolence loose on me.

"Never grow old," he said, laughing. I couldn't help laughing with him. "Thanks," I told him.

But when I turned from his unsynchronized gaze, she was halfway up the hill, running, running.

A night a month later. Though I had managed to finish some old work and had put a handful of days in on Miss Neihardt's story, I finally let it slide. The writing seemed schizophrenic, part of it a hyperbolic fan mag kind of prose, eddying in other places in long-winded ruminations I had no right to. Reading it over, I realized I had left off writing about her and started in on myself, venting my own broodings through her life. What it needed was another long interview, but I'd put off going for a week, then two. I sat at the kitchen table, afflicted with a free-floating edginess, my thoughts crowded by the clamor of people's confessions, the voices dovetailing into a mean-spirited chorus.

She was in bed, as she was every night by eleven, her perfect teeth flossed and polished, cheeks scrubbed, her sleep posture assumed. In her catechism the imagination does its sublime work early in the morning; she took pains not to miss it. No lying awake mulling for her, no skewering around under the covers, no waking me with lousy dreams. I'd bent and kissed her and come out to have a friendly glass of beer with myself before joining her, but now there were were five cans dead on the table, and one more had rolled off onto the floor. My imagination did what it wanted to. If something memorable turned up, I was willing to be astonished by it—a fool among fools. Lately the harvest had been lean. I got up and stared out the back window. The nearby houses were all dark, the sky above them cramped and starless.

The kitchen looked pitiful. Every stain and scratch seemed to stare back at me. Things were out of plumb, counterfeit. There on the Formica was a glass baking dish of yesterday's peach cobbler, an uncharacteristic effort of hers toward domesticity. I tried a fingerful, but it was sticky sweet. I turned and suddenly slapped the beer cans away. They clattered across the grimy linoleum like spent shell casings.

I stood in the middle of the room, rubbing my face. The beard seemed to lay crossways on my cheeks and my fingers felt like chalk.

"What in hell are you doing here?" I asked myself out loud.

The voice sounded like a drunk's, but the man who answered, inside, spoke clearly.

You love this woman, he said. *You think that's true because you never loved anyone before. You've never felt chosen, you never had the pins knocked out from under you. You've also never been so unsure of what you were doing. She says she loves you and you repeat it to her like words in a foreign tongue. You've opened your house to her—you've changed your life. But isn't something wrong?*

I didn't believe it. I ground sparks into my eyes. The stillness was awful. Something snapped then, and the anxiety charged out of me like a cloud of acrid chemicals. I knocked over the chair I'd occupied earlier—an antique I'd once stripped of pink paint, sanded carefully, rubbed with linseed oil, given two even coats of sealer—but instead of righting it, I hoisted it overhead, pausing slightly to get my balance, and brought it down on the rack of dinner dishes, sending shards of china twirling. Then down on the plants lining the sill, the clay pots shattering in the sink, the snapped vines dangling from their pins. Then down, full-bore, on the peach cobbler, spraying mangled fruit on the faces of the cupboards. The legs splintered and came off, along with the seat, leaving me a handful of smooth slats that I beat into the table until they were kindling.

She was in the doorway by this time, wide-eyed, barefoot, smothered in a checkered flannel nightgown.

I dropped the last stick, and it barely made a sound.

"Is there an explanation for this?" she asked.

"Explanation?" I repeated through heavy breathing.

I knew she wanted most of all to be reasonable and, maybe later, understanding. But I saw that I'd disturbed her, shocked her even. I had blind-sided her, touched a weakness.

In an instant, seeing her hug the doorway like that, I understood how important it had been that we know each other only in our strength, in our artful design. I got a vision of her history: one of those rare girlhoods as smooth as new ice, unmarred by rapid thaws or flash freezes, across which her skates left a trail of indelible grooves, the strokes as regular as breath; a youth that left her certain, with no need of looking back. The only mystery for her was the future. Before my eyes, and hers, she was reduced to an ordinary, baffled, run-of-the-mill human being. And I knew that I should love her all the more for that. I should have run over to her and swept her up and stomped around the kitchen with her, laughing, crunching on the broken pottery, until we were weepy with our fallibility, then waltzed her down the hall to bed. But I didn't, and we didn't, and finally, without budging from the doorway she said crisply, "No really, I would like to understand this."

The drizzle was upon us. The screens beaded up silvery and cold. I felt like a mammal with a hard winter at hand. In our valley the sun disappeared for months at a clip, taking with it our ability to stand up tall and see things from a distance. Through the north window, above the empty typewriter and my mug of cold coffee, the snowline was unmistakable on the mountains, lower than yesterday.

She knocked lightly on the door, a courtesy she had never observed.

"I'm not disturbing you?"

"Course not," I mumbled, already disturbed.

"Hanna," she said. "There's a few things I haven't told you. Not that I meant to be devious, but I didn't know how you'd feel about it, so I waited until I was sure."

It was a balancing act; her composure made me squirm.

"About what?"

"All right. I'm going to Phoenix."

I wished then that I hadn't gotten up to face her because her eyes offered me no chance to think. She made Phoenix sound like the moon.

She tried a smile, but it seemed to die crossing the space between us. "I'll be working with a new design group. Probably, I don't know. . . ." She sheathed her fingers in the waistband of her jeans, " . . . three months. February maybe."

For the first time in as long as I could remember I was free of pressing deadlines and could have gone anywhere with her, but there was not the least bit of that idea in her voice. She was moving on, to put it simply. What surprised me most was that I could be surprised by it.

"It will be good for me," she said.

"Of course it will."

"The air is wonderful, the sky over the desert. . . ."

"I've *been* there, I know all about it," I said, a fraction sharper than I had wanted her to hear.

"I'm sorry, Hanna."

"What is it you want from me exactly? Permission?"

"There are just things," she went on—as if she'd already explained it to herself, repeatedly, in just these words—"that are necessary, that are *crucial.*"

I couldn't look at her any longer. She touched my back.

"I don't want your permission; I want you to understand."

And that quietly we had taken the first lesson in being strangers again.

Still, there were a few good days. We went around pretending nothing special had happened, though in odd moments we checked each other for symptoms, listened for declarations. She stripped the walls, packed her leather bag, laid her other things in an army surplus footlocker that—since it wouldn't fit in that fast little car of hers—I hauled down to the Greyhound station.

We made arrangements. We would skip Thanksgiving but meet for Christmas halfway between here and there. And after that it wouldn't be long before she was home with me. Or so we said.

The last night we shared a steak for two at a lodge on the foothills road. Huge logs burned and tumbled down in the fireplace. Molly sipped a ritual glass of wine as I worked the bottle down, then another. We didn't have much to say, so we settled for the dinner, the surroundings. Across from me in the firelight, she seemed to flicker, there and not there.

She waited for me in bed. She had always been an aggressive lover, but that night there was desperation in her moves, as if she were the one getting away. It went badly. I was dopey with the wine and dispirited. I fell quickly asleep and dreamed my foolish dreams.

I woke instantly the next morning, and she was gone. Awareness surrounded me like an electric field. There would be no message, no lipstick kiss on the bathroom mirror (she didn't even use lipstick), no last sentiment taped to the milk carton. Room by room I went, taking my time. The more I didn't find her, the more my missing her became a thing I could grasp. My empty hands led me back to the bedroom, to the debris of blue linen. I found myself wondering if she'd even spent the night. It seemed to matter a great deal—a piece of necessary detail for the record. Did she lie there imagining the steps she would make through the dark house, did she already feel the cold leather and anticipate the exact moment her headlights would fade into the day? Did she hover over me, finally, testing the depth of my sleep?

More things I would never know. I made the bed and shuffled down to the kitchen and fixed some instant coffee and dosed it with Benedictine. I sat at my desk and drank, but it did nothing for the cold lump under my ribs. I wondered what other men would do. Could I have made a heroic stand? I hated the timid fiction we had settled for. I hated our failure to admit we had no future; and I hated us for not turning passion into anything that could grow and multiply and last. I tried to work. My fingers were lifeless, but in a few minutes I wrote: *In the closing shot of* The Harvest *you see the young widow scything wheat against a background of mountains touched by early snow. Her jaw is set, her eyes are steadfast and black, declaring her refusal to mourn, to squander pity on the dead. It is a look you remember, having once seen it, when you are tempted to spend pity on yourself.*

I left the paper in the typewriter, made myself presentable, and went out to talk with Miss Neihardt.

The time went by like so many summer reruns. I neither invited involvements nor discouraged them. In an age of high romance, I lacked flamboyance; in an age of hustle I failed to intimidate. The women I dated thought I was a nice man. My friends, though they had been startled by her presence, soon forgot Molly and considered me chronically solitary. As I once had, I accepted their judgment. Whatever the reason, it never happened to me again.

I gave up reminiscence for brisker subjects, did the life of a hockey player and followed that with the story of a running back whose career the sports press called *meteoric*. It had been that: the night before the play-offs he'd shattered his kneecap in a high-speed motorcycle accident. His was a tale of the '70s: the ghetto kid who parlays his singular talent into college, into the NFL, a staggering contract, the cover of *Sports Illustrated,* a two-thousand-yard season—all of it brought to ruin with a single unnecessary risk. His agent had signed him for the book, and at the taping he was sullen at first and talked as if he'd memorized his own publicity sheet. My questions irritated him, but he finally understood I wasn't there to expose him or to glorify myself. Finally I turned off the cassette and asked him, "Why take the chance?"

"You feel superior," he said. "You feel like they can't touch you, almost like you stopped being human, and started being . . . I don't know, something else. Sometimes you can't stand it. Sometimes you say to yourself, *OK, Jack, let's go for a ride, let's unload some of this shit. . . .*"

I did my best. His book came out in paper, adorned with a glossy shot of him crossing the goal line in midair. We never met again. I saw the book at the checkout counter of the supermarket and in the wire racks at the newsstand downtown, each week a row closer to the floor until it was gone.

More recently, for good money, I've turned screenplays into paperbacks known as novelizations. I hole up in the screening room for a day and watch the film over and over until it seems perfectly inevitable, empty of surprises. I take the script and a box of colored stills and drive up along the ocean and check into my favorite kitchenette, a room with a view of the water and no interruptions. I lock the door and tape the pictures to the walls, in sequence. Sometimes it takes as long as two weeks to pound out the book version. I only let myself think about what shows on the screen. My metaphors are workaday.

This time it is different, though: not a potboiler or a big-budget disaster picture. I bought the rights myself. The director was well-known, but the film never got much play. The critics who liked it called it *close to the bone* and said it *radiated a cold brilliance.* Those who didn't said it was *hermetic, grim, cryptic.*

The story line involves two middle-aged lovers who cannot seem to get quit of each other. Can't or won't—I've tried to decide if this is, finally, the same thing. I'm disturbed by it. That I have even chosen to work with it is disturbing. I can't put it at a safe distance. Their arguing is an inexhaustible frontier. I can't write a word. For days their faces surround me. His is stern, always ill at ease: framed now by a car window beyond which the landscape looks cratery and burned; now at a beach in the off-season, his eyes retreating from a sardonic smile; now a closeup, frantic sobbing. And hers: Nordic, fair; in the first shots she strains to make an expression that is normal, reasonable: later the elasticity is gone and there's only one look, shot after shot, and it says: *Thanks for stopping before you killed me.* I want to talk to their images. I walk the beach in thought. I come back, can't face cooking, send out for Chinese food, then let most of it get gummy in the carton. The story can't be changed. It stands in front of me, solid as an obelisk, yet untouchable as a mirage. Foolishly I've taken down the pictures and tried rearranging them, tried to find an image of satisfaction to put last.

It is this she has walked in on.

We stare at each other. I'd tell her how wonderful she looks if her coming weren't so cruel. Still I can't back away. Compared to me she looks so little changed I wonder if even the first sight of me is enough to make her bolt. But slowly our smiles cleave and grow in light increments. We are mindful of the remaining distance between us. We savor the hesitation before impact.

"You're not so hard to find," she says.

In late twilight we walk the hilly outskirts of this town we are strangers in. We stop in the fireweeds, and she takes my hand. Across the road a man and woman are building a house together. Their yellowing trailer sits nearby, watched over by a chained Husky that has worn a half-moon of ground bare by its door.

Blows from the woman's hammer echo through the empty neighborhood. We watch her arm rising and falling against the blue light. The husband fires up a Skilsaw, and it tears through a row of two-by-fours, the butt-ends falling away one by one. The blade-guard clangs shut, followed by a deep silence. Framed in their lattice of dark studs, the two figures move together, twin hearts in a rib cage.

"Are they happy?" Molly says in a minute, the old earnestness in her voice cut with a soft unhurried sound. I look at the couple who have resumed their work and imagine the walls and insulation filling in around them, the rooms growing full of people who belong to each other.

"Are you?" I ask her as she turns to me.

All the way back to the apartment I am light-headed with worry, about who she is and how we'll manage the static between our bodies. When I turn from the little icebox tucked under the counter, she has taken off her shirt and stands gold-skinned, hands cupped at her waist, unsorrowful, a look of mock-impatience crossing her lips.

"Well," she says. "You remember how?"

We roll around in the bed like nineteen-year-olds. The first hour is fantastic, broken by laughter and rushes of unexpected energy. Still, we are alone in it, I think, each of us back somewhere in our unspeakable thoughts—a couple of old parents watching their children rough-house in fallen leaves. I get up later and switch on the light over the bathroom sink and leave the door cracked, so that her face will not get away from me. I hold her as she sleeps.

When I wake in the bright morning, she is there. Holding her tea cup close to her chest, she follows the photographs around the room, politely, as if in a gallery. She looks up and asks, "Who are they?"

"People," I tell her. "Just people in a movie."

She sits near me. She talks of Denver and Key West, of Paul the pilot, of Willy who wanted children to leave his successes to, of commissions and prizes, and of me. Strangely, I have no jealousy for all this other life sunk in the middle of her story like a pool, around whose edges I'm only a sometimes visible shadow to her as she swims.

"I'm sorry," she begins to say once, but I won't let her. There is no time for that.

She shuts off the water and comes to the middle of the room. The dress slips over her head like the fluttering of many wings.

"Where will you go?" I ask.

She smiles, sitting beside me in this little bud of blue light.

I am suddenly present again at all the times I've wanted her, the odd moments, between towns, between thoughts. Maybe it is, after all, my failure to tamper with her story that she both respected and couldn't settle for. Maybe it was her acceptance of me into her lovely vision that I took for love. Or maybe it is foolhardy to try to track it all down.

Like Some Distant Crying

The first thing Celestia sees is how the beard grows down across his heart, ragged as dried sage. His long-jointed hands are full of kitchen knives he clatters on the counter before looking up at her.

"Hope you don't want nothing to eat," Murphy says.

Celestia stands in the glare of the west-facing window, inspecting the insides of this runty cafe she has come to after thirty miles of bad road. The ceiling is low and warped into graying pastel waves. Forest Service maps cover the walls, smudged where travelers have located themselves, then their destinations. There is a glass case with a few bobbers and lures and a sparse filling of junk food. At one time, she can see, a pool table stood at the far end of the room, where now there is only a rectangle of varnished wood.

"A can of Coors beer," Celestia says. "Nothing to eat."

"You alone?" Murphy squints past her, the webbed skin puckering around his eyes.

"Alone."

Murphy waves back a seamy strip of calico and shuffles into the kitchen. Over the icebox a glutted fly-strip twists in the feeble breeze of an electric fan. He bends and picks out two cans and holds them to his white shirt with his forearm as he replaces the open padlock on the icebox door.

Celestia sits on a red vinyl stool and wipes the dust from around her eyes. She is long-limbed and fair, with high, smooth cheekbones and a blonde braid coiled twice around the crown of her head. The clothes are khaki surplus and big on her. Only the soft lines and the discipline in her face suggest she is no longer a girl.

"You do them," Murphy says, shoving the cans at Celestia. "I'm sick of cutting my damn finger." He waves a hand at the screen door, at everything on the other side of it. "Crazy people," he says.

Celestia takes a long, cold swallow and wonders if the man will go into a complicated speech on the subject of modern life, but Murphy returns to the knives, lining them biggest to smallest along the counter. He spits into the center of the whetstone and rubs it with his finger.

"I thought this was a hot springs," she says.

"At one time," Murphy tells her. "You're late."

"There was a sign out on the highway."

Murphy works the blade in tight little circles on the stone, stops, and tests it across the back of his liver-spotted hand. No blood yet.

"I'll admit the paint was half off it."

Murphy checks her closely, seeing what it is he is dealing with.

"Nobody around here bothers," Murphy says. "Not for a long time."

"Show me."

He wipes his hand on a rag and turns to the room and decides it can likely get by without him for a few minutes. Celestia follows, out the side door and down a path by a row of whitewashed, closed-up cabins.

"Hunting season," Murphy says. "Used to rent them out."

In the shadow of the last cabin, Murphy halts and peers into a rabbit hutch. A dozen or so sealpoint bunnies doze inside, hyperventilating in puffy balls. The only other life around, Celestia guesses, figuring that even an old shade dog would be too much company for this man.

"You like rabbit stew?" he says over his shoulder. He leads her down to a wooden enclosure sitting flush to the slope of the hill, overgrown with red willow and rosehip. He unwinds a strand of fishline that holds the door, steps back for her to pass.

It is not pretty, not what she expected—though generally she tries to expect nothing. Inside the plank walls lies a square pit of pebbly concrete, surrounded by flat paving stones, and long benches furry with moss and smoldering lichens. An iron pipe extends through the far wall, crusted at the mouth with whitish minerals, a trickle of water weeping from it. Sometimes there's a grace in what no longer flourishes, but she doesn't feel that here. This decay is acrid, not at all nostalgic. Hugging her arms, Celestia looks into the pool. The water is a foot or so deep, brackish, clumps of algae floating in it like spoiled hamburger.

"You make a big mistake," Murphy says, "thinking things ain't going to change." He has come close enough to talk low, but he keeps his eyes from the water.

"What happened?"

"I'll tell you," Murphy says, *"Underground,* who knows what goes on?"

"You mean it stopped?"

"You best believe it stopped." He twists his beard into a tattered point. "Most likely a tremor of some kind, way down."

He checks the sky, but there is nothing to divert him, no hawks, no evening swallows.

"You know it's down there somewhere, but there's not a blessed thing you can do. If it decides to come up somewhere else, then it does. It could shoot out anywhere or nowhere, it don't matter. And praying don't help either."

"That's kind of sad."

"Sad?" Murphy says. "I'll tell you what's sad."

He goes to a small door by the feeder pipe, bends, and disappears. Celestia strides after him. In the moist shadow stands a column of concrete that houses a heavy-gauge iron valve, and Murphy is staring at it sternly.

"You do it."

Celestia wraps her fingers around the cool wheel and pulls until, abruptly, it gives. She can hear water behind her gushing into the pool.

"Then it come back on."

Forgetting him, Celestia steps out to gaze at the clear water chugging from the pipe, watching with fascination as it falls and knocks the algae away in trembling rings.

"Now you seen it," Murphy says. "Turn it off."

"Why?"

"Just shut her down."

Celestia heeds the edge in his voice, and when she has shut the valve Murphy checks to see that it is tight, then walks out.

Spears of gold light come through the old boards, catching him in his tracks. His forehead glows like soft fruit. "It just come back on sometime," he says. "I don't even know when. I was walking down there on the road one day and saw the hill was all wet where it was spilling over. It was a terrible mess in there. I hadn't been inside there for years. . . ."

Murphy's voice has turned impersonal now, his words a kind of recitation.

"So what's so sad," he tells her, "what's so goddamned sad is, I'm too old to care."

Celestia watches him wave his hand at the whole of it.

"This here," he says. "One time it was the back door to the kingdom of heaven."

The next afternoon she is back, having spent a dreamless night in an air-conditioned motel down by the highway, carrying a bulging rucksack and a brown paper bag of groceries. Unsurprised, Murphy squints up from the chopping block where he has sat down, arm-weary and dispirited among the debris of larch chips.

"What is it?"

"I want that last cabin," Celestia says. "That one by the rabbits."

Murphy shakes his parched face from side to side. "You don't want to do that," he tells her. "Them cabins are filthy."

Celestia smiles patiently, not a natural attribute in her, but something hard-won. "I don't think you ought to tell me what I want."

"It won't do."

Celestia adjusts her grip on the food sack.

"Out of the question," Murphy says. "That's all done with. I don't rent cabins."

"This is different," she says, turning now, not for the gravel drive where her canvas-top Jeep is pulled into the long shadow of the ridge, but for the path to the cabins. Murphy shouts after her once, but the voice breaks up like so much steam.

Celestia lets the sky in, lets the air circulate. She pumps water at the kitchen sink, washes down the linoleum counter tops, sweeps dust and mouse turds and flakes of gray bark from the floor of the front room. She wipes out a cabinet and lines it with fresh paper and unpacks tins of sardines and tuna fish, and when she is done she crosses the streaks of sunlight and sits on the front steps, watching the empty road twist up the draw along the river, and there below, the square of rough-cut fence that hides the pool, the afternoon turning slowly blue around her and shading into evening.

Later, in the dark, she unrolls her down bag on top of the mattress, smooths the wrinkled nylon with the gentle distraction of a woman straightening a small child's hair. She sits on the edge of the bed, wondering if she has done the right thing this time. For a long time, momentum has been all she has had: roads like ever-branching capillaries, no reckoning the number of miles. It is hard to give it up, even for rest, even for the strongest taste of destination she has had in months.

You can't run from your history, she has been told more than once. It sounds wise and time-honored, but she has realized, watching the sun-burnt landscape pass by the plane of her windshield, that nothing that has happened should be grieved over more than is right, nor its pain worshiped. Her boy is dead. He is buried and life has resumed, though so changed it seems to her like another life altogether. Her husband was broken by their loss, a weaker man than she had ever expected him to be. As the course of the boy's illness veered into inevitability, he could give nothing, not even, in the end, acceptance. He craved and demanded the comfort she had to give to her son. And afterward, he bolted to the tenderness of other women, leaving her to face up to the world on her own—which, months later, she sees as a kind of blessing. Her choice was movement instead of bitterness. Hot water to hot water, she has worked her way through the northern Rockies, trusting the driving to keep her alert and forward-looking, trusting the water to temper her spirit.

She lights the kerosene lamp finally, risking a visit from the old man; and soon he is at the door, on the pretext of bringing wood, though the few sticks rattle in his arms. She lets him in, shows him that there is enough wood for a fire if she wants one. Murphy peers uneasily around the circle of light, as if he is the stranger. It is surely not the same here. There should be rifles resting in their cases, loud laughter, detailed accounts of stalking deer and elk. It should seem more haphazard and temporary.

"I don't like it," he says, coming to what has stirred him out of his own kitchen. "I don't like you being down here alone."

"I'm plenty used to it," she tells him.

"It's spooky."

"Sure," she says. "What isn't?"

"I don't like it."

"I don't need your worry," Celestia says, her voice as paced and nearly friendly as she can manage. "If that's what it is. But I don't think it's me you're worried about. Tell me if I'm wrong."

"A woman shouldn't be out here alone."

She faces him, composed, self-sufficient, telling him plainly: *It's all right.* But she knows it is difficult, that a woman alone is an agitation and a threat. She never meant to be alone, but now that she is, she pays attention to its demands, and one of them is knowing the difference between pity and fear.

She crosses to the table and lifts the lantern, and Murphy's shadow shrinks up into him.

"I'm going to blow this out now," she says. "Please go."

In her dream that first night, Celestia sits shoulder-deep in a pool of hot water, enclosed by a ring of grassy hills. The sun glimmers low in the sky, trapped in a smear of clouds. She feels the familiar buoyancy in her breasts. Her arms float before her, the fine blonde hairs dirtied by shreds of brownish moss. She hears the clicking of hard smooth stones, looks up to see a small boy walking the edges of the pool. How pretty he is: round shiny cheeks lightly rouged with windburn, hair like cornsilk idling in the soft wind. He stops, looks out toward the center of the pool where Celestia waits, perfectly still. He does not see her. She wonders if she can call to him. He moves on, walking the perimeter, now and then peering again into the drifting stream.

Early the next morning Celestia discovers that Murphy hasn't bothered opening the cafe. She turns from the locked door and notices that the gate to the pool is cracked open and goes down and finds him head in hands on one of the old benches. He has not heard her come up, and she sees how he is: alone, a face rinsed in terror. She comes closer and sits cross-legged, and he doesn't speak for a long time, except with those pebbly eyes that keep saying: *Damn you girl, what are you doing here?* As if her presence is exquisitely ill-timed, an intentional cruelty or, worse, something he might have earned by living wrong.

The air is crisp with Indian summer; long shadows divide the cement into clean chunks of light and dark. Murphy points finally to the far end of the pool, to the exposed steps.

"They all come here to get healed."

"I know, yes."

Murphy's eyes say: *What do you know!*

But soon he goes on. "Carloads of them. They drove up from the city and went in there and took their clothes off and come out in those godawful black sacks and they sat right there, turning pink, all of them expecting some kind of damn miracle. I can see them in the shallows, so many shriveled old things, all eaten up with old age. Summer or winter, didn't make no difference. They'd close their eyes, and it was like they left their bodies behind. I was just a kid then, and it scared the hell out of me. Just a kid."

"Who knows what helps?" Celestia offers.

"It don't matter what they thought," Murphy says. "They were still old and there's no healing that. And let me tell you, it was more than once we found them belly-down and half-parboiled. My old man had great plans for this place, but it all went to hell."

Murphy grunts. "I ain't running a place for dying people, you hear?"

He glares at her as though she has demanded this information of him. And though she has not felt young in a long while she knows that Murphy takes her for a girl, holds that youth against her like mortal sin. She could go chapter and verse with him on death, but she won't.

"Why'd you hang around then?" she says.

Murphy looks to see if this is an accusation or what. "Some of the boys got called off to serve in the army, but I didn't ever and I pretty much just stuck it out here."

"Why is that?"

Murphy shakes his head. "I'll be damned if I understand a bit of it," he says, as if a display of ignorance explains anything. It reminds her, for a moment, of her husband.

During the night the sky has streaked, each successive wave of cloud coming lower and more dense until the stars are gone, and Celestia wakes to a drizzle redolent of moss and dying leaves. She sits upright in the mouth of the mummy bag, watching her breath disperse into the weak light, adrift. It is not so bad a feeling.

This day the cafe is again closed, and Celestia wonders if it was simple chance she ever found it open. Murphy is nowhere in sight. Celestia pokes around and notices that the truck is gone too and hopes this is his day to go for supplies. She walks to the pool and ties the door behind her.

The air smells like mushrooms; the rocks give a dull luster. She circles in the cold mist, looking at this hole in the ground. The stillness is humbling. She rolls her pantlegs to the knee and steps over the edge into the cool water and wades to the center, dead algae dark and slippery around her calves. Through the sole of her moccasin she feels for the depression where the drain grate sits. She squats in the murky water and feels how the metal is swollen with calcium and layers of organic residue. She begins working holes in it with a screwdriver, until she can feel water swirl around her fingers.

In an hour the pool has drained to a thick mulch: pine needles and aspen leaves, rusted cans, window screens, a rotted bench. Celestia drags tools from a storeroom off the bathhouse. She begins scrubbing the side walls with a long-bristled broom, later takes a snow shovel and plows the debris into ridges on the floor and carries it away a shovelful at a time. All day the light rain keeps falling. She stops late in the afternoon, drenched, resolute.

She climbs out and sees what she has only half-consciously surmised close-up. On the bare floor, in a white paint that hasn't flaked like the blue background, someone has painted the ponderous reclining figure of a woman. Though exhausted, Celestia smiles: it is as unreal and tasteless as it is wonderful. All the thoughts she has kept away with work wash back over her as she sees the painted figure, image of all she is and is not.

She has not heard Murphy return, but nearing her cabin she finds him at the hutch, stiff and silent. The suspenders cross his white shirt like streaks of rust. He stares at the bunnies as they twitch against the wire mesh. He opens the little door and takes one by the loose fur of the neck and cradles it to his ribs, turning finally to regard Celestia, who has stopped a few feet off, her clothing wet and filthy, her face glowing.

For an instant she sees him as he might have been in whatever prime he had. Maybe it is just the eyes, the way they alone are unaged and pay no credence to the frailty everywhere around them. There is a coldness, a flicker of power, and she is caught up short.

"I know what you're doing," Murphy says.

She nods.

"Don't you take me for a fool," Murphy says. "That would be a mistake."

"It's nothing to do with that."

"I won't let it go on," he says.

Celestia keeps her tongue. Murphy rummages with his free hand under the hutch and pulls out a scarred bench and hunkers down beside it.

"Come here," he says over his shoulder.

Celestia balks at this.

"Down here," he says. He turns and grabs her hand and draws it down until it squeezes into the fur of the bunny's neck.

"Soft, ain't it?" Murphy says. From the shadows he retrieves the longest of the knives, its edge fully restored.

"Don't act surprised," he says.

"You do it right in front of the others?" Celestia says.

"It's as good as any of us get," he says, and before Celestia can pull away he takes the knife by the backside of the blade and runs a quick noose around the rabbit's neck and jerks back on the ears, exposing the sucking windpipe and severed tips of the arteries.

It is sickening, but she cannot move. How different and triumphant the blood must seem to him. When the body has stopped jerking against the bench, Murphy stands holding it by the back legs and lets it finish draining in silence. His shirt is soaked through and adheres to his skinny ribcage. Beads of rabbit blood cling to his beard. As Celestia watches, the full sad weight of his age discovers him again.

Sometimes the loneliness calls with a cold whistle, and she can do nothing but hear it. She remembers how it is to fall away from her husband's body and lie on the strewn sheets as he sleeps, the passion gone like a tide, the room steeped in an autumnal mood. And she remembers how it is to kneel at the level of a small boy and read in the pale eyes the first intimations of terror—and nothing to say that will help, but saying it anyway. There is no part of it she can forget, but she will not give it dominion.

The morning of her third day she goes straight to the pool and begins hand-scrubbing the walls and watches with a burst of pleasure as the paint emerges clean and sky-colored. Soon only the floor remains and she rests, knowing that Murphy will not return to the spring on his own. The privacy pleases her. The sky threatens to clear; a light breeze riffles the firs. She feels her second wind come on and begins the floor, cleaning with broad luxurious circles of the brush.

By sunset she has given the pool a final rinse. She secures the drain and cranks open the valve and stands by as the first thin waves skate across the cement. She has seen stronger springs than this—but still it's good, plenty hot and abundant. The painted woman shimmers. Though there is no face—only two blue gaps which regard the sky indifferently—her presence is unavoidable. Who knows what the man who painted her saw: mother, harlot, sister who strayed and was lost to the world? Women standing in relation to men, a heavy, clumsy symbol for a generation of aging bathers. And who was he: Murphy's father, Murphy himself? Celestia's attraction to the place is harder to name, but for the first time in a long while, she feels at home.

Later, from the cabin steps, she can still hear the splashing beneath the pipe mouth. She lets the darkness fill the air around her until she is invisible, waiting for her strength to return in the lulling company of her thoughts. Lights are burning in the rooms back of the cafe, now and then blotted by Murphy's pacing. The windows are open and if Murphy stops long enough he will surely hear the water too, like some distant crying in his ears.

She knocks lightly on the screen door and walks in. Murphy is at the table by the window, staring at a drinking glass full of steaming water, a tea bag hovering above it at the tips of his fingers. He cannot seem to drop it in.

Uninvited, Celestia sits in the other chair and folds her hands on the bare wood. "What do you see in that crystal ball?" she asks him.

Murphy lays down the tea bag and tries to snap back an answer aged in brine, but it dies in his throat and he just shakes his head.

"Don't see nothing but meddling," he says finally.

"I'll bet you were a real killer when you were young," Celestia says. "Were you tough as nails?"

"I was all right."

"I'll bet the girls couldn't stand it."

"Girls . . . ," Murphy says. The memory seems fragile, collapsing to dust as he touches it.

"Why don't you leave an old man in peace," he says.

"What peace is that?"

"I was all right before you came. Now I don't know. I lost my place."

"What are you afraid of?" Celestia says.

"I know what you think," Murphy says, for the first time looking at her full. Her composure stops him for a moment. "You think you know about me, but it don't matter what you think."

She waits.

"You think you can come in here and take over and tell me what's good for me. But I'll tell you something, you ain't going to change nothing here."

He drops the tea bag into the water, a cloud of amber swirling to the bottom of the glass.

"One mother's all a man needs," Murphy says.

Celestia doesn't bother smiling. All her life she's heard talk like this. "You think I'm doing any of this for you?" she says. "You think a woman's heart is full of pity?''

She stands to leave him, looks down at the tangles of gray hair, the knobbed fingers, at the whole stubborn solitariness of the place.

''You missed it altogether,'' she says. ''This is for me.''

She doesn't wait now, but turns at the door and speaks back to him. ''Drink your tea, old man,'' she says.

The rabbits wake, sniffing and edging to the recesses of their hutch as Celestia walks past. Inside the fence, she lights two lanterns, the Coleman she brought in the Jeep and another from the cabin. In her absence the pool has filled. Mist rises from its surface in luminous twists.

Celestia undresses and slips her body into the hot water. In a life stripped of other ceremony, this could do just fine. She glides in the dark, free of gravity, free of solid ground. In the heat, her body seems to merge with the water. Often as she has felt this sensation—in one spring after another—it never grows any more safe or familiar than anything godly ever does.

She jerks her head into the air and breathes, turns and floats on her back, arms outstretched. When she opens her eyes again, she sees that he has come, as she knew he would have to, and that he stands quaking behind a veil of steam.

''You can't make me,'' Murphy says.

Celestia drifts closer, the water glistening like oil on her skin.

''You can't force me,'' he says.

But she doesn't want that—not force. She is no world beater, nor a victim. Her power is only to know herself, the power of water rising from where it is trapped underground to nourish what is parched.

Murphy stalks the boundaries of the pool, hands empty but clenched as if still holding knives.

''I won't *allow* this,'' Murphy says.

''Of course you will,'' Celestia says, spinning closer. ''You know you will.''

As long as she is in the water there's nothing he can do to her. She is in no hurry whatsoever.

''What is it?'' Murphy says. ''What do you want?''

Celestia stops where she is, near the shallow end, and stands, the water line around her ribs. She is silvery and sleek in this light, though she is of no mind to taunt him. He will have to get used to seeing her in the water.

"Stop fighting," she says. "Stop fighting what you can't fight."

Murphy clutches at his beard, futilely. "You don't know," he says. "I couldn't bear it anymore. You don't know what it was like here. They were all dying, every goddamn one of them, suffering and dying, and me nothing better than death's pimp. I was too young for that."

"Listen to me now," Celestia says. "You and I are the living. That's the only truth of it. Come."

She extends a hand.

The suspender droops from his shoulder, his fingers fuss with the buttons of his shirt. Then he is naked and spectral, walking slowly to the far steps and down, through a lifetime, into the water, until it rises around him and finally holds him up. Then, his tears indistinguishable from spring water, he takes the first strokes toward the center of the pool where Celestia now floats, skulling a gentle circle.

Morning Practice

Kate heard nothing when she woke. It was not the absence of shouting or laughter carrying through the big house, but of her mother's cello. As a girl, waking in this bed, she had heard her mother practicing in the room below, the sonorous climbing and falling of the scales and etudes, the oddly appealing scratch of the bow, come rising through the wide softwood flooring. The music would be broken now and then as her mother paused and leaned toward the music stand, marking the score with a stub of pencil, her head tilted for her bifocals, or when she took a breather, her eyes drifting to the finches on the feeder, then closing in brief reverie. In the disturbance of first waking, Kate thought it was one of those small, distantly familiar silences she heard, soon to be overrun with music.

But her mother was dead now. Kate peeled back the cold quilt and sat up. The daylight was bloodless. She set her feet down onto the floor. She was Kate Wolf again—since her divorce—home to be with her father in his grief. Gerhard, seventy now, would be downstairs in the kitchen, his single egg and muffin eaten hours ago and the dishes done. She hoped she would not find him staring out the back window as she had several mornings, his fingers whitened against the sash. She hoped he had slept.

The first nights after her cremation, he had refused sedatives. He had not slept well in recent years. *I don't know if it's insomnia outright or what*—Kate's mother had written once—*or if he'd just rather. He'll kill himself.* Her mother had often sounded that way, irked and protective at once. Now Gerhard acted as if he could get by with no sleep at all. By day, the grief was a stubborn mass he, by turns, faced like a gentleman and shied from as if it were numinous and charged with powers. At night, it broke to pieces and pursued him. But he would never call it grief. "I'll be coming to terms with this thing before long," was all he said. She had never in her life seen him pitted against anything that could not be managed—yet, she was not sure. She had her own sadness, though she found her worry for Gerhard distracted her from it. After dinner each night he slumped in the leather chair opposite the kitchen fireplace, holding a glass of Scotch against its padded arm, nursing it. His feet splayed out as if anesthetized. For hours she watched him—never getting drunk, never nodding off.

Kate, like her father, was drawn to the fireplace, but neither had heart enough to bring it to life. She heard a faint acrid whine in the flue. It was too easy to see her mother tending the fire, poking at the hickory or beech or ash with a kindling stick, abrupt, almost careless—in such contrast to her movements over the cello. The whole room was too full of her, but there was no place else for them to be. The house beyond was drafty and overlarge. Kate turned on the radio and twisted the dial to a big band show. Jack Teagarden, Paul Whiteman. It was not her mother's kind of music, but she remembered that Gerhard had liked it. Mildred Bailey sang "More Than You Know." Gerhard's eyes rose and trailed the lyric across the air, then fell away as if fooled by an accidental flicker of light. They talked a little, indirectly, as if they were strangers caught in the same slow line. *You don't cure anything with talk* would have been her mother's firm opinion. Maybe that was right, but she wished they would talk anyway—Gerhard was all she had now and the time dragged. If her mother had been a woman of baffling disciplines, her father was simply a moderate, private man. He drew his lips into a small stoic smile. "Katie, where's the reward in it?" he said, but it was no invitation to pour out the heart.

So each night he outlasted her, standing with an air of damaged formality, urging her to take her rest. "I'm fine now," he'd announce, hands buried in his chino pockets, shoulders drooping. "I believe I'll turn in a bit later." Kate would stretch up to kiss him and their cheeks would brush lightly. Then she went up into the dark part of the house, already nettling herself for things she had not said. The room did nothing for her discomfort. It had been hers, surely, but now it was no one's. Her mother had kept no archives of Kate's girlhood. It was redecorated quietly—Audubon prints, pastel drapes, twin beds with matching lamps. But, lying awake, Kate heard the easterly wind catch at the eaves, a soft wincing sound that sliced through time. In the big storms of the past, the hurricanes and three-day snows, the eaves would howl, waking her and leading her to the cold sill to look down scared, the turmoil outside balanced against the house and her solid, sleeping parents. She remembered that, even if the room was scrubbed of her.

In the morning, Gerhard would look awful, his eyes like a hound dog's and his hands shaking as he smoothed back the long strands across his bald spot. Kate would ask again if he'd take the pills, her patience toughened each day as he declined. But finally he accepted them, though Kate took no credit; more likely it was that his modest nature had finally become affronted at what had become of him. It was stuporous sleep, only a break from his thoughts, yet it was a start. A month had passed. The Indian summer was played out and the sky hung like dirty insulation. The field grass in the morning was frosted in pale random arcs. Her father slept, without help. He looked more like himself, more the way she remembered him.

There was no talk of him leaving the house for other quarters. He would stay, despite its rambling size, despite the emptiness of its rooms. Nothing else made sense. Gerhard had sold his business eight years earlier, with some fanfare, as if embarking on a new unburdened episode of life. What had their plans been? The first year to be spent in Italy, Kate remembered: time enough for the great music of Europe and time enough, she supposed, for them to tend each other. Her mother must have described it, but the letters blurred. How much she'd craved such a change of scene, Kate never knew. Her own life had been bright and accelerating then: a new husband and career, two quick promotions, all on the far coast of the country. When the retirement came, though, her parents stayed home. Why had they not gone? She flushed to think she never asked. Gerhard had turned his attention to the house, renewing the effort he'd begun over thirty years before, restoring and renovating it room by room. Surely Kate's mother worried about him, about the effects of isolation and inertia on a man so long busy with commerce. But she needn't have. He worked methodically, attending to the old wood, absorbed in the monotony of plane or handsaw—not so different from her, practicing every morning in the music room.

He would stay, but he would need to find a new way to live there. When Kate found him in the music room that morning, she guessed this was what he was mulling over. It occurred to her that this was probably the first time since her mother's death that he'd been in there; maybe it had been a lot longer than that.

"I feel like a trespasser," he said.

"I know," Kate said, touching his sleeve. "I feel it, too."

"You spent more time in here than I did."

Kate nodded. It was a room that soaked up time. One fall, Kate had granted her mother's wish and studied piano there, working her way without flare through the John Thompson method books, before she was allowed to drift back to her natural pursuits: tramping at an idle pace through the pine woods beyond the field, down to the granite quarry and its bottomless water. She had no head for the rhythm. She remembered her mother standing by the piano bench, slapping her tiny waxen hands together beside Kate's ear, sometimes actually catching it between them as she counted the beats aloud in love and impatience.

"She kept it so *bare* in here," Gerhard said. "Wouldn't you think she'd want a little . . . something, color?"

The walls were a plain white plaster, the wide flooring deeply burnished by years of dark wax. It was a room suited to Grieg or Sibelius, yet she hadn't liked them. *Gloomy men,* she said. *Life's sad enough.* Her taste ran to Telemann, Vivaldi, Mozart, the chamber pieces. Sometimes she'd allowed herself the dreamy introspections of Mahler. The music stand was empty. A straight-backed chair stood before it, empty too, except for the gold sweater draped over it. Gerhard ran his fingers over its stitches. Kate wanted to reach out and take his hand away and lead him out of there, but she balked, and was then struck by what had seemed so wrong about the room.

"Where's the cello?" she asked him.

Gerhard looked dazed. His eyes darted around, found nothing but the hard case standing open in the corner like an empty sarcophagus.

"Beats me," he said.

Her death came freakishly. On a Monday night in September she went out to the porch where Gerhard was watching the Red Sox on the portable, and told him she felt tired and was going up to bed. By Wednesday she had consulted their doctor and found she had pneumonia, a mild case it appeared. She rested. Thursday it exploded, drowning her lungs in fluid, taxing her heart. By Friday the infusions of Keflex had had little effect; suddenly, she was gone. Gerhard, on his way from home, had been a few miles from the hospital. He'd called Kate once earlier.

"Should I fly home or anything?" she asked him.

"You know how hearty your mother is," Gerhard said.

Kate had never thought of her as hearty. Strong, yes, but not robust. Strong in another sense. "Can I call her?" she asked.

"They have her tranquilized," Gerhard explained. "And full of tubes. Maybe they'd let you talk. I don't know."

Kate had tried that night, but with the difference in the time it was too late. When Gerhard called again, late Friday, with his awful news, he did not reach her. Kate was just beginning to date again, warily. She had been to a show with a young lawyer named Rudy, had enjoyed both him and the evening. She marveled at this privately and asked him back for lunch Saturday. She took her father's call standing in her sunny kitchen cooking eggs. Gerhard went on and on and the kitchen lost its coherence. She listened, trapped in the sunlight, in Rudy's benign expectant smile. Her breath caught in panic.

Flying home, she was haunted by the call that had not gotten through. The plane's wing cut through the empty air like a cutlass, its light blinding, but she could not bear to look around at the faces of her fellow travelers. She could not remember the last time she had talked to her mother. It had been a couple of months, and what had they talked about—nothing. But her mother had never talked to her at length about anything. As a girl, Kate had dreaded the speeches her friends' mothers had made them sit through, but they never came—not the one on boys, not the one on self-respect and independence, not the one about how the daughter would only understand the mother's feelings when she had children of her own. Her advice, when it came, burst out in cryptic fragments. It horrified Kate to think of dying suddenly, with no chance to clean up after herself, but if it was any consolation it wouldn't have horrified her mother. Once Kate had stumbled onto her crying at the back window—her mother had spent the morning with Kate's debilitated grandmother at the nursing home in Peterborough. "Live your life, Kate," her mother said angrily. "Live it and be done with it." Kate had not understood, except for the chill in the words and to remember them years later.

Toward the end of her long flight she wept off and on. She was tense and tired but had composed herself by the time she walked out of the tunnel into Logan to meet her father.

"When we were kids," Gerhard said in the car, talking freely at first, "well, it happened all the time. You don't know how it used to be . . . it was dreadful. You got pneumonia, you lived or you didn't live, it just depended on how strong you were. But now, who's heard of it anymore? There's no sense to it." By the time they were out in the country, though, solemnity had overcome Gerhard. His voice stilled, like the clotting of a wound.

It was no surprise that Gerhard had forgotten what had happened to the cello. It was accidental, unrelated, though looking back, Kate read it as an inkling of catastrophe and knew somehow that her mother had seen it that way, too. One morning late that summer she'd played quartets in Lancaster. Troubled as she sometimes was with bursitis in her shoulders, she'd chosen to carry the soft case that day. When the playing and the lunch and the talk were done, and she was preparing to stow the instrument in the car's trunk, she was interrupted by her friend Mary Louise asking for some sheets of music that lay in the back seat. Her mother retrieved them, met Mary Louise halfway, talked a little more, then slipped into the car and backed out over the cello, crushing its neck under the rear tires.

All this she explained to Gerhard, and once he'd called it back into memory (later that day, over the kitchen table) he offered it to Kate. His voice was deadpan, the details flattened and disembodied. But Kate had no trouble imagining her mother's recital: her lips stretched taut as tomato skin, her head giving frequent bristling shakes. Her moods tended to contradiction: at one moment, near-saintly reverence for all creation; at another, brooding spitefulness barely kept in check by her breeding. Only after Kate had married and gone away did she feel equipped to study her mother. By then the urgency had worn off. She listened to her father now and knew that he suffered from the same long-standing puzzlement.

"Of course, I offered to get her another," he said. "But that one was, well, you know how long she'd had it. It played a certain way, I suppose. You know her hands weren't very big."

Kate remembered. Her mother had sometimes put her palms up against hers, telling her *What I couldn't do with hands like yours,* which always licked at Kate's guilt for being so little persistent with the music. But now she smiled to herself as she thought of her mother's hands pressed finger to finger with hers, and then the smile embarrassed her and she let it fade.

"Couldn't they fix it?" she asked her father.

Gerhard's gaze kept slipping off toward the willows beyond the window. The leaves were brittle and fell with every twitch of wind.

"Dad?"

"I'm sorry," Gerhard said. "We talked about it, I think, but I'm afraid I don't remember what the verdict was."

"What would she do with it? Did she have someplace she always took it?"

"Lord, Katie. I don't know a thing about that."

"It wouldn't be so hard to find," Kate said.

Gerhard was slow to respond. "I don't know," he said. "Why don't we just let it rest."

"No, really . . ." Kate said.

Gerhard shook his head, so Kate backed off. It wasn't worth

threatening the progress he'd made. In a moment he excused himself. Kate sat by herself a few minutes and finished her coffee, looking out at the shivering willow and the fields and the somber sky. It was enough to make *anyone* melancholy. She cleared the table and washed the dishes, thinking about each dish, one by one, and nothing else.

Later she went upstairs and listened at her father's door. She cracked it and saw that he was napping. Even in sleep his brows arched quizzically. She drew down his shade and tried to tiptoe back across the uneven floorboards without disturbing him. She hesitated by the bed. His long body was pulled up awkwardly, exposing his calves. They were blue-white and smooth as potato shoots. She wished her mother were there to tell her how to take care of him. She had no knack for it, even when she'd had a husband of her own. She spread the comforter up over him, but as she leaned to his face he stirred; she moved her lips away abruptly and drew back.

Turning to leave, she saw Gerhard's dressing table, silver brush and comb, finger-smooth bowl of tie tacks and whatall, everything ordered and talc-scented. Her eye was caught by a dark, half-curled picture tucked into the beveled mirror. It was her mother as a schoolgirl—her eyes hard as chestnuts, her sack dress drab and its bow fallen, her thin arm draped coquettishly about the neck of the improvident instrument she'd chosen for herself. Kate had never seen this. She looked back at Gerhard sadly and nearly ran from the room.

She went straight to the music room then and began looking for a receipt, a scribbled address—anything to go on. She found drawers of music, old strings fastened with rubber bands and new strings in their paper slips, tuning pipes, hard dusty splinters of rosin with traces of bow hair—nothing at all to say what had become of the instrument to which these things had belonged. Worse, it struck Kate that there was nothing personal there, not a picture of any of them, not even a concert program. It was as though her mother had shed her identity at the door. Kate went quickly to the kitchen phone and tried the yellow pages, made a few calls in the area, then tried Boston. The men she talked to had stubborn European accents. She could not be sure how well they even understood her—no one had seemed to recognize the name. She slipped the phone book back into the drawer, the despair coming on in prickly waves.

She woke in a start the next morning, surprised to find she felt good, full of energy, quit of recriminating dreams. Overnight the idea of finding the cello and bringing it home had turned to a sharp hunger; she wanted her father to share it. She smiled to herself in the mirror as she drew soft black lines across her lids. She had not bothered with makeup for days.

Downstairs, Gerhard went through the motions of protesting, but she knew she'd caught him at a vulnerable time, his morning chores over and his emotional posture for the day still up in the air. She handed him his jacket.

"Let's make the day a good one," she said.

Gerhard smiled wanly. He is trying, Kate thought.

She drove. She took the back way, always a more agreeable road than the highway, but as they neared Concord she saw that the farmland had given way to huge tracts of condos and bright franchise stores. The roadside she remembered was quiet and dusty, shaded by hundred-year-old sugar maples. There had been fruit stands now and then—she remembered hugging her mother's side, mystified by the deep shadows, the smells of the produce, her mother's bartering. It was a road both she and Gerhard had traveled often, but long ago, and even then, seldom together.

Gerhard was silent until then, sitting primly on his side of the seat. Black knit tie, tweed coat, hands folded in his lap except when he raised a finger to rub the groove on his nose his glasses made. He spoke up suddenly, his voice modest as a boy's.

"Katie, I'm sorry you never had brothers and sisters."

"I don't mind," Kate said, surprised.

"I know, you never complained. But still, it's a loss."

"Really," Kate said, "I never dwelled on it. Maybe it was better this way."

"When your grandmother died, it was a great comfort for me to have my sisters," Gerhard said. "And. . . ." He shifted uneasily on the seat, allowing his eyes a quick check of the road ahead. "Well, the truth is that sometimes I think it was terribly unfair of us to withhold that from you."

"I always thought it was more a *medical* thing," Kate said. "I thought they told her. . . ."

"She was old for it, that's true," Gerhard said. "It's not an easy thing to explain, Katie. You were such a blessing to her, I think she felt she couldn't risk it again. She was good with you, she was always there . . . if you could have just seen her. But it was almost too much for her. She . . . couldn't seem to relax."

They had begun down the long last hill, the Boston skyline laid out before them like a bank of grey ledges and the sea beyond it a streak the color of wet bark.

"I wouldn't have minded a bigger family," Gerhard said. "It seemed only natural to me. And we had the big house. But then." He seemed just now to notice the city around him and to straighten himself as if it called for decorum. "I'm sorry to go on like this," he said.

"No, it's fine," Kate said. "I'm interested." But she did not pursue him. In bigger families, it seemed to her, all the children's curiosity turned the parents public and legendary, but she had never supposed her rights were unlimited. Alone, reared in the civility of their house, she'd shied from the space between the generations. For the first time that day, she got an intimation of the trip's risk. Yet, she was still buoyed by its prospect. Above all, the cello was real and tangible and she wanted it.

The shops were like their owners, Kate thought. Some were obsessively neat, not showing a scrap of planed wood; others were musty and painstakingly Old World, the Beethoven spilling from speakers buried somewhere deep in the clutter; a few others gaudy and commercial, overstocked with brilliant guitars, mandolins, fiddles fitted with electric pickups. In each place Kate explained their mission. No one knew a thing. She and Gerhard crossed the river and moved deeper into the city.

"See Isaacs," they told her finally. "He'd be your best bet."

"Isaacs," Kate said, jotting the address down on an old deposit slip in her purse, trying to think if he was one she'd called.

Gerhard said nothing about the day's wasted energy. He walked along beside Kate, almost dutiful, eyes upturned to the height of the buildings, like a stranger to the city. The day had darkened prematurely. The columns of offices and apartments along Commonwealth absorbed the sky's sooty light. The people walking toward them hunched into a headwind. Kate took her father's arm. She spotted Isaacs's sign finally; it was discreet but flaking, directing them to the third floor. She smiled. She drew Gerhard inside. The stairs were dim and worn slick, rising before him like a tunnel toward a splinter of light. The weariness raked across his face.

"Come on, then," Kate said, helping him forward, past the moment. Gerhard started up the stairs. Kate took his arm again, but after a couple of steps he stole it away from her and climbed by himself.

Isaacs proved to be a man of her father's age, though shorter, with a puggish face and a full head of black hair swept back over a broad head and wetted with oil. Disorder overwhelmed his shop. A hooded lamp shone over the workbench, but Isaacs was loitering by the window, a viola arrested halfway to his chin as he stared out at the snowy sky.

He glared over the tops of his glasses at them. "What is it?" he said, intruded on, but a moment later softening to their presence as possible customers.

"Mr. Isaacs?"

"Come in, yes. What can I do?"

"Excuse me," Kate went on. "We think a cello might have been brought to you. My mother's. Mrs. Wolf."

Isaacs abandoned the window and came to them, suddenly thoughtful. "Didn't I talk to you?"

Kate avoided Gerhard's eyes. "I wasn't sure if I made myself clear," she said.

Isaacs eyed his workroom. Everywhere lay pieces of instruments, clamps, tall wood vises, a long rack of bows on the wall like a waterfall of horsehair. In the far corner the light failed and there were only glints of carved wood here and there. The accumulation seemed archeological; Isaacs's look said there was nothing odd about instruments being left there and settling into the strata.

"And this was when?"

Gerhard leaned back against the workbench, silent.

"August," Kate said.

Isaacs nodded. He stroked his jaw, his fingers set like calipers. "I don't know that name," he said. "You could look around. You'll be cautious, of course."

Kate believed he meant it, so she slipped around the counter and made her way toward the back, stopped then, and saw that her father had not yet budged. Isaacs had migrated to his side and tried to engage him in talk, and when that produced only a tip of the head Isaacs held out the viola to him. Kate watched her father stare down at it, then politely, silently, refuse it.

Isaacs shook his head, startled to find someone within the doors of his shop who was not a string man. He tucked the viola under his own chin and plucked a run of low reverberant chords.

It was hard to distinguish among the dark instruments arrayed on the back tables, but shortly Kate caught sight of it: her mother's cello. It stood by the window, not a foot from where Isaacs had been as they entered. Kate knelt to it. The neck was still broken, but she hardly cared. She clutched it up and rushed it back to them in her arms, her pleasure girlish and severe.

"Here," she said. "This is hers."

Isaacs let the viola droop away from his chin, studied her a moment, then the instrument.

"I'm sorry," he said. "That can't be. I know all about that one. It belongs to an old customer of mine."

Kate laid it on the table before them. It was no larger than a small body. She turned to her father. How could he not recognize it? Couldn't he see it in her hands, and see her wearing her long black skirt, her hair done, her rings off—and with that, see the two of them, father and daughter watching her perform, proud to see her shine in public, but as much outsiders as anyone in the audience? Gerhard didn't move.

"I promised her a loaner," Isaacs went on. "But I haven't heard from her. It does seem strange."

"Who is it?"

Isaacs smiled enough for Kate to see the gold scalloping along the bottoms of his front teeth. "Well, I'll tell you, she lives way out in the country," he said, with a sharp wave of his hand, as if everything beyond the old heart of the city were still wild and uncultivated. He glanced from Kate to Gerhard, then back.

"Emily McBride." He shrugged. "I don't know any Mrs. Wolf."

Kate's father reached his hand out and touched the cello. His finger left a line in the fine dust of the sounding board. His eyes crimped. "Yes," he told Isaacs. "My daughter is right. This was hers. She was my wife." His voice was harshly matter-of-fact. "She gave you her maiden name, it seems."

Oh, yes, she would, Kate thought. The sound of that name filled her with a burning logic, the understanding of which she had put off for years. Her father said no more. Kate pressed between them looking back and forth between their two old sets of eyes—Gerhard's like pale water-washed stones, the old luthier's dark as knot holes.

"She died, I'm afraid," Kate said, not wanting her father to have to explain anything. "It was right after she brought it here."

Isaacs drove his hands down into his apron pocket. The heavy flesh of his face bunched with the news. "Such a *loss,*" he said. He looked up and let his eyes roam the shop, as if to acknowledge that death was a frequent visitor, that it came and breathed eternal stillness into the instruments where they lay. There could be no doubt that Isaacs had known her, in a way they had not—and that even now he was recollecting her story of the accident and his own sympathy and his welcoming of the broken instrument. And Kate knew that her mother had never told him about a husband or grown daughter. In Isaacs's shop she had no other life.

Emily McBride. Kate Wolf. Who were these women with their maiden names? Kate thought of the picture on Gerhard's mirror and she thought of the mother she remembered: absorbed in her morning practice, the fierce concentration as she worked over the hard places like an abrasive until they were smooth as air, her mastery over them the outward coefficient of a struggle that had gone on within for years.

Had Kate really thought they would all rest more easily if they found the cello and brought it home? Had she thought that finding it would be akin to finding her mother? Kate's shoulders clenched, as if seized from behind. What lay in front of them was shabby without its strings. The ebony was gritty and splintered, the scroll-work crushed like stale icing. It was as empty of her as it was of its scouring music.

Kate turned to her father. He was weeping. "She had her private ways," he said. "Didn't she. Didn't she have her ways."

Gerhard was poised just above collapse. She put her hands on the back of his jacket and hugged him to her. Slowly, he drew up his arms to her shoulders.

"She didn't mean anything," Kate lied. "I know she didn't."

Isaacs stood apart with an awkward tenderness, his pain mingled with confusion.

Kate smoothed the hair along her father's temples—it was so fine she barely felt it. The self-reliance, the stiffening against hurt, the pledge to love without collapsing and suffocating each other—had Gerhard ever known how fiercely his wife had held to such principles even into death?

You have me, Kate whispered.

Isaacs came to the table and lifted the broken neck gently where it hung, testing its weight in his hands. "This made a lovely sound," he said. "Such a loss. I can't tell you. I could work on it if you'd like. . . ."

Kate straightened herself. "It's nothing," she said.

She took her father's arm in hers and eased him back from the table. At the door she stopped and turned to Isaacs, who had not taken his eyes off the cello. "I'm sorry," she said. "Do whatever you ought to. We don't belong in here."

In the dimness of the hallway the steps down were treacherous, but Kate held her father firmly, and they made their way out to the darkening street, unaccompanied.

Home Fires

Longer than anyone knows, fir and tamarack had clung to the sharp slopes of the canyon, ravaged by lightning fires and bark beetles and gravity, their tenacity witnessed only by the moody northwestern clouds, by birds of prey whose serrated wings bore them on the tricky thermals, by families of deer carefully following trails beside the fast gray water. In this century Jeep roads intruded until the entire eighty miles could be traversed by a strong rig, though it was never thought of as a way to get from one place to another. Then in the 1960s dynamite and giant earth-movers left a two-lane blacktop highway that matched the river's twists, ascending in places hundreds of feet above it through unguarded switchbacks.

It was an early morning in the dregs of a September that had frosted early. Scattered stands of aspen and weeping birch fluttered in the shadows. Down in the heart of the river, kokanee salmon were making their first run, a few now to be followed by great numbers, swimming upstream toward the waters of their spawning—surely it was a kind of miracle that they should ever find their way back, no longer feeding, their bodies already soft and pulpy in preparation for death.

Traffic on the highway was sparse, relieved of the sluggish flow of motor homes and top-heavy camper outfits from other states. A few feet past mile marker 44, where the road climbs into a smooth northeasterly bank, a fresh pair of double tire tracks continued straight that morning, through the chunks of reddish clay, into the dry brush and the feathery upper branches of the firs.

The truck lay upside down, back end crushed like a soda can, cab folded into so dense a bolus of steel it would take Search & Rescue better than two hours working with welding torches and hydraulic jaws to discover it contained no body. Up slope, scattered among the outcrops of shale and limestone, in the trees and resting here and there on the flaps of freshly gashed topsoil, white packages of frozen fish were strewn, still rock-hard, though the exposed sides would feel mushy to the fingers of the first county deputy to huff down the slope, midafternoon. The truck had nearly made it to the river, stopped only by a slug of granite twice its size, where now the man named Pack squatted, head between his knees, glancing up every few seconds at the wreckage.

He could not understand why it did not include him. He should not have survived such a mistake, should not first have made it. He tried to picture the night just elapsed, the route that had led him to the lip of the road. He had no precise memory of it. Surely he had fallen asleep. Drivers fear the graveyard hours, though that fear is so close to the heart of what they do that it remains unsaid. They ride behind the wheel, pumping Dentyne or cigarettes or Maalox, half-thrilled by the power of the diesel and the reach of the headlamps, half-terrified by their limitations. They flick cassettes into the tape player and set the volume so high the treble jars them out of that dreamy hypnotic mood that comes just before the moment their heads drop. They sing, they banter with one another on the CB, they juggle weights and distances and velocity in their heads. Anything to keep them sharp until it is light again. In the end, though, the fear itself provides the energy.

But Pack was never like that. Driving those hours he found a kind of peace, a solitude that was its own reward. The darkness outside seemed to illuminate his loneliness, seemed to tell him it was only the natural way of the world. He aimed the passenger mirror inward at his own face so he could watch his eyes in the halo of dash lights. He never used the radio except sometimes to tune in an all-night talk show from the coast and listen to the paranoia and longing that gave the voices their peculiar timbre. He kept to himself at the truckstops, letting his cup be filled and refilled as he watched the other drivers kill their nights off under the acid lights. He would be privately pleased when the phone would ring and the waitress would wipe her hands and grab for it. It would never be for him.

He could not remember choosing to be a driver. He had fallen into the pattern of it a job at a time, found it suited his disposition. He had been to college but picked up nothing lasting there except the taste for reading, another solitary pastime. Sometimes on long nights he thought about his wife, but it was in the same drowsy distant way he thought about what he had read. He did not doubt that he loved her, but he could not remember choosing her. She had been with him as long as he could recall—the adolescence she'd marked the end of only a blur now, dotted by occasional points of shame and excitement. When he came home to her, his desire quickened and he'd hold her and listen to her deep sure voice and be happy, but driving again, at night, he knew that the two were not one, after all, but two.

Pack sat on the crown of the boulder, surrounded by the quiet and bird songs, trying to make sense of what had happened. He saw himself popping out the driver's door as the nose of the truck first hit, his body flipping backward through the branch tips, pitching like a dead weight into the snarl of laurel where he'd come to.

He ran his fingers up and down his legs, over his ribs and back, finally touching around his skull, searching for the fatal exception to his good luck. Though he was dizzy and his forearms were devilled with long scratches, he could find nothing dreadful.

He climbed off his perch and bent over a sheltered pool. His face was thin and droopy-eyed, fringed with a beard the color of clay dirt. His eyes were the blue of an undeclared predawn sky. He smiled into the calm water, and it was then he saw that his front teeth were gone, ripped out by the roots. He touched the gums delicately, felt the clots forming over the holes, withdrew his hand, and saw the fingertips evenly stained, as if his body were nothing but a bucket of blood.

At that moment the sun first crossed the ridgeline and Pack squinted up the steep slope, bathed now in keen September sunlight. The dizziness gave way to a rush of clarity, as if he'd only now begun to wake up, not just from the accident and from the night, but from ten years of living in the dark. He looked at the crumpled truck, the torn earth. Clearly he was supposed to be a dead man.

He knows his loneliness better than he knows me, Elisabeth Pack, called Willie, wrote her sister who had moved east. *Maybe I am a jealous woman after all.*

She put her pen down, stared impatiently out the side window where the two pear trees had dropped their yield into long sweeps of grass. The leaves were brittle and gold. The road dead-ended here. If there had been children, it would have been a safe place for them to play, away from the hazards of through traffic. But there were none. In the distance, the parched foothills hung in a blue morning haze, curving out of sight toward the mouth of the valley where the river flowed wide and tame, accompanied by the tracks of the Burlington Northern and the placid interstate.

But I doubt it, Willie wrote.

She was a handsome woman, six feet even—slightly taller than Pack—with clear hazel eyes and soft lines around the mouth. At thirty she wasted no time mourning the woman she was or might have been. In uniform her presence was striking. Intensive-care patients were guarded by her skills, comforted by her manner, perhaps mistaking her reserve for serenity or for a larger, more merciful view of things, one in which the sick always healed and the grieving were granted peace. It was good consuming work; with Pack gone so often she was happy for it.

His homecomings have become unbearable, she wrote, frowned at the words and stopped. It was not exactly what she meant to say. She preferred her letters to remain simple and full of news; even in the ones to her sister she was seldom confidential. She was embarrassed by the heaviness of her words. The fact was, though, his returns *had* become more difficult to cope with. She had long-ago accepted that Pack—for all her love of him, for all her willingness not to judge him—was a man who came and went. In the ten years of their marriage he had gone off on the fire lines their first summers, after that had shuttled rental cars back to the Midwest, traveled with a bar band called *Loose Caboose,* and in recent years driven truck on the long interstate routes.

He was always edgy just before he left, and she would have to turn away from him to avoid a fight. He always returned with a high-spirited exhaustion, coming to her bed for a spell of love-making, hard and wonderful for Willie, though lasting too long now, leaving her body sore and her spirit cut by resentment. She saw his passion soon spoiled by restlessness, as if she were not an object of love but of release. It had not always been like that, but she had to admit, privately, it was now. Still she forgave him that. What worried her more was that even between jobs he seemed to come and go, as though tracing an elliptical orbit around her and the part of his life that remained fixed. Sometimes she believed he might swing too far, snap loose, and keep sailing out into space.

"How do you put *up* with it?" her friends sometimes asked over coffee.

"I don't see that it's really a problem," Willie said, willing to defend Pack from loose talk. She could handle the Pack whose nature it was to come and go, who hadn't settled into a life's work the way she'd imagined he might, who seemed an odd character put up against their husbands. But she knew they also meant: *How can you trust him to be faithful?* Faith was private, Willie thought. It irritated her the casual way her friends rated their husbands' performance, almost eager to see them fail and at the same time scared to death of losing them, especially to someone else. She was not afraid of losing Pack to another woman.

Once she told him: *I don't mind sleeping alone.* "No?" Pack said, smiling at the darkness, rubbing her wide damp stomach. She had meant that it kept her from taking him for granted, that the emptiness of her bed, at night and again in the morning, stayed with her as a reminder even when he held her and warmed her. And she meant it as a kind of triumph, too, because it had not been easy for her at first; she had needed to learn to be alone.

Unbearable, she had written.

She craned her neck and squinted through the white sunlight at the clock on the kitchen wall, saw that it was already afternoon. She finished the letter quickly, dismissing her remarks as a morning's bad humor, sealed it, and laid it by her purse.

Though it was still early, she grabbed her uniform from the hook back of the bathroom door and slipped into it. She sat on the edge of the bed and double-knotted her white-polished Clinics, rising then for a quiet inspection in the big mirror. She liked to see herself in the white uniform, her wheat-colored hair drawn smoothly over the ears and gathered in a silver clip at the neck. She liked not worrying about the quirks of fashion, but more than that, the whiteness itself pleased her.

She closed up the house and walked out to the Volvo and idled it lightly in the driveway, a kind of nervousness overtaking her, the feeling that she'd left something undone. The afternoon light seemed suddenly frail, as if this were the exact moment the season turned. Her thoughts about Pack troubled her. She wished he were here, she wished he could walk down the hospital corridors beside her, feeling what she felt: the terrible precariousness of the lives and their links to one another. She wished he understood that.

Veins of worry began to dart through the halo of bright amazement surrounding Pack as he studied the ruined truck. The tires pointed absurdly in the air, splayed and flattened; the painted lettering emerged without meaning from the jammed aluminum. Unignited gasoline mixed with freon from the fractured cooling unit and gave the air a gray stink. It was pasttime for precaution, but Pack was overwhelmed with being too close. All the sounds he had missed in his flight now swarmed into his ears. His stomach balled up like a fist.

He backed along the silt-caked stones, hands tucked into the tops of his jeans, staring at the wreckage as it diminished and began to blend with the other debris along the river. He walked upstream until the current bent sharply around a deposit of harder rock and he could no longer see the truck, kept walking a long time, the click of the small hard stones ringing in the narrow canyon. The roadway was high above him, out of sight; he wanted no part of it.

When he stopped, the sun was nearly overhead, its light broken into rich shadows by the low-hanging limbs of the cedars. As he knelt he felt the shakes coming on strong. He got up again quickly and caught the glint of orange rip-stop nylon, across the river and a short ways up a feeder creek. Above it rose a thin braid of smoke, the first sign of life Pack had seen. He waded into the shallows, the water rising over his boottops, then out where it was deeper, bending his knees against the current. Approaching, Pack saw two women crouched by the fire, for the moment unaware of him. The one facing him was slight—*wasted,* his wife would have said—even in a down vest. She pulled her blue stocking cap down over strands of pale hair as she leaned to flip a pair of fish skewered above the coals. The campsite looked small and orderly. The other woman, who had been sitting back smoking, head down, suddenly caught sight of Pack and grabbed up a shotgun he'd not seen resting beside her.

"Hey!" Pack said, freezing.

The woman aimed the gun at Pack's midsection and appeared willing to squeeze off a shot.

"There's been an accident," Pack said, hands lifted in a victim's posture.

"There could easily be another," the woman said. "You alone?"

"No trouble," Pack said. "OK?"

The woman in the vest got to her feet and squinted at Pack's face, turned, and shook her head at the gun. Her companion slowly lowered it until it pointed at the pine needles around Pack's feet.

"Tell us what happened," she said.

Pack moved in gingerly, squatted, and told them what he could remember. "I was headed home," he began. It sounded like somebody else's story, though the throbbing in his mouth reminded him it was neither made-up nor borrowed.

The women seemed to listen with special attention. Finally the one with the gun cracked a smile, but it was thin-lipped and made Pack more nervous. "It should be that easy," she said.

Pack looked at her, not understanding, not knowing what to do next.

"Here," the other said. "You want some food?"

Pack shook his head. He was beginning to feel truly bad. "You think it would be all right if I maybe laid down?" he said.

The women checked with each other. The one in the stocking cap nodded toward the tent. As Pack stood she caught his arm and said, "Let me . . . ," dipping a corner of her towel in a pan of hot water, then dabbing at the blood dried around his mouth.

"Don't you get weird on us," the woman with the gun said. "You understand?"

Pack nodded. He crawled heavily into the tent, slid across the warm nylon and collapsed, watching the leaf shadows twitch above him.

While Pack slept the truck was spotted by a young man who had stopped above the ravine to photograph the eagles circling above the salmon run. He trained the long lens of his Nikon down the embankment, scanned the river bank for signs of life, and wondered what the little squares of white were. After a while he walked back to his van, dialed the CB to channel 9, and began calling for help. He was joined eventually by two county deputies, the highway patrol, Search & Rescue, and the coroner. The photographer followed the police down to the wreck and stayed until the light failed, snapping pictures of the truck and the broken slope and the faces of the workers, listening to their speculations, pleased to be so close to it all. The plates of the truck were checked through the Department of Motor Vehicles and identified. In Pack's darkened house the phone rang every hour, beginning at dinner time, continuing late into the evening.

Pack woke abruptly and saw that it was fully dark. It seemed as if a great flood of time had swept him away. He thought for a moment that he had dreamed but realized what he had seen and heard was the power of the fall itself, magnified and reiterated in the stillness of his mind. He ached everywhere; his lips and gums were swollen hard around the missing teeth. Peering from the tent flap, he saw the woman who had cleaned him sitting alone by the fire. Pack joined her. She smiled in an easy, sisterly way. It was as if they had gone in and studied him as he slept, reading into the man he was and deciding he was not a danger to them.

"Rita believes these are desperate times," she said. "She believes it's important to be armed and ready. Are you any better?"

"I don't know."

"That was a miracle," she said.

"I don't know," Pack said again.

She laughed, her cheeks glowing round in the firelight. "Any fool could see that."

"Kyle . . . ," Rita said, breaking the circle of light, armed now with a load of firewood, her voice reedy and careful. She knelt and dumped the wood, looked back at the two of them.

"Kyle," she said, "what have you told him?"

Kyle stared into the flames. "I just told him it was a miracle."

"Yes, that's true," Rita said. "But what will he do with it?"

"I don't think he knows yet," Kyle said gently.

Rita dusted the wood flakes from the front of her sweatshirt, then stooped and poured coffee into a tin cup and handed it to Pack, its steam puffing into the cold air. Pack nodded and took it, and it felt good between his hands.

"They'll be looking for you, of course," Rita said in a minute. "They'll figure your body fell into the river and was carried downstream. You could have gone several miles by now. It's not uncommon. For a while you'll be called missing, then presumed dead."

She stopped a moment to let that sink in. Kyle moved closer to Pack.

"I was missing once," Kyle said, quiet excitement in her voice. "My husband looked all over for me. No telling what he would have done if he'd found me. He'd done plenty already."

"Beaten her," Rita said.

"At first I was hiding upstairs at the hotel with a wig and a new name. I didn't know what I was going to do exactly. I couldn't sleep. Sometimes I could see his truck going down the main street and one night I saw it parked outside the Stockman's Bar, and he came out with someone else. I wasn't surprised. The next morning I took the bus to Pocatello."

"Yes," Rita said. "He was a bad man. A real prick."

Pack heard the tinkling of a brass windchime hung in the tree, drank his coffee in small careful sips.

"Still," Rita went on, "Kyle was smarter in the heart than I was. I waited until I was barely alive, barely able to help myself. But all that's changed now, as you can see."

"Can you eat yet?" Kyle asked Pack. "I saved a fish for you."

She tugged a bundle of tinfoil from the edge of the coals.

"You'll need strength," Rita said. "Whatever you decide."

Pack took the fish into his lap and cracked it open and lifted out the long limp spine and tossed it into the fire. The meat crumbled in his mouth.

"But you're not a bad man, are you?" Rita said.

"What do you think?" Pack asked her.

"I think you're a lucky man," Kyle said. "But luck's only the start of it."

"Let me be blunt about this," Rita said. "They will be looking for you, but they don't have to find you."

As she spoke she stood behind Kyle, her fingers lightly stroking the shoulders of the down vest. The smoke twisted up before them, through the fringe of trees to a wedge of sky overcome with autumn constellations.

"Brother," Rita laughed, "have a new life."

Right then Pack stopped chewing and looked hard at the two women. *"New life . . . ,"* he said.

"Clean slate," Rita said. "Maybe you have the nerve, maybe not."

"I don't know," Pack said. "I can't tell you exactly how I feel."

"That's right," Kyle said. "That's how it is at first. You feel sick."

"You get this unmoored feeling," Rita said. "But then you start to see destinations and you go ahead." Her soft white face shone with patience. "Don't tell me you wouldn't like another chance."

Pack was silent.

Rita stood over him a moment, then said, "Now, we're going to bed. You can stay with the fire as long as you need, but it's going to be very cold here soon. Believe me."

Passing by, Kyle whispered to Pack, "Don't think it was an accident," and disappeared toward the tent.

"Thanks," Pack said.

He stayed watching the fire until the last cedar log burned through, showering the air with fine embers, stayed remembering the fires of his life, the blue-gray smoke of branding fires and the stink of burnt hide, the scattered fires of his childhood. He stayed listening to the steady clamoring of the creek, imagining the water's descent, how it wept from remote snowfields, came together, and followed high country drainages to the wide rivers that passed under the city's bridges disappearing west toward the sea. He thought of all the lighted places where he had stopped, the extravagance of his curiosities, and the careless ways he had broken faith with his wife. When he bent later to crawl into the tent, he heard the powerful contentment of the women sleeping. They had left one bag empty for him and were together in the other, holding each other like twins. Pack backed out and stood alone in the cold, measuring the foolish turns his life had taken.

The phone back in its cradle, Willie Pack let her uniform drop to the linoleum of the downstairs bathroom, wrapped herself in a terry-cloth bathrobe, took the Valium bottle from her purse and carried it to the kitchen, lit the gas under the tea kettle, stared at the clear blue flame until the water steamed, turned it off, and sat finally at the breakfast table, surrounded by the bright enamel, the saffron scalloped curtains, lacing her long fingers together in front of her, sure that this moment of control was a fast-fringing lifeline.

Save your tears, she could hear her mother saying. As a child she'd imagined great fetid reservoirs of unshed tears. *Save them why?* How lame and remote her mother's efforts were. Yet Willie knew, perched in the solitude of her own kitchen, that she had grown so much like that woman, believing life was best treated with caution and reserve, believing that loved ones could suddenly trade places with darkness.

Missing, the sheriff had stressed, his voice like fresh gauze.

All her life she'd wanted the exact names of things. Beneath his words she heard this: We haven't found a body yet—in country this wild we may never.

"What does *missing* mean?" Willie said.

"Anything's possible," the sheriff said. "I'm sorry."

"Thank you," Willie Pack said.

So in that time before the confusion and the shouting and crying took possession of her, she held her own hand and rested in an aura of clarity not unlike the one that had settled around Pack hours earlier, as he contemplated the boundaries of his good fortune. This is what tears were saved for.

She had long-ago accustomed herself to his absence, but though it looked the same as always it was not. She felt a flush of shame, to think she had ever enjoyed having him gone. Solitude meant nothing if it was infinite. She thought about death, the way it was taught to her in school, the predictable steps the minds of the living and the dying took in confronting it. Month by month she practiced its sacraments, sometimes finding in her discipline an antidote, mostly not. The farm wife died whispering: *Tell them. . . .* The twenty-year-old logger witnessed the bright splashing of his blood with a pure and wakeful knowledge. She heard the halting voices of old husbands turn suddenly eloquent in the white hallways, reciting an Old Testament catalogue of suffering and accommodation.

She thought then of Pack's missing body. She remembered the feel of her fingers sliding down over the arch of his ribs, she pictured his beautiful hip-swinging gait through the downstairs rooms, the angle of his fingers resting across this table from hers. The image of that body torn and broken rose in her like a searing wind, bringing a wave of sadness—for Pack's body having to die so far away and alone.

She drew a long, controlled breath. For the first time since the telephone call she forced herself to see Pack's face, straight on. It was then, in a burst, she understood what she'd hidden from herself: that she had not seen Pack as he actually was in a long time. What she saw now was not the face she had guarded in her imagination, the one she had married as a teenaged girl, the one she had always reckoned her own happiness by. What she saw now was a face with eyes crimped and glazed, a mouth constantly biting at something, a thumbnail or an emery board or the inside of his lip. It told her Pack had been missing long before this night.

She lurched to the sink and threw up and kept heaving though there was little in her stomach except the dark residue of cafeteria coffee. She ran the water and watched it swirl over the grate, gradually washing away her nausea. In a few minutes she straightened and snugged her bathrobe.

She spilled the blue pills on the table, spacing them evenly with her finger, imagining the sleep they would bring, each one clarifying it like sudden drops in the thermometer, until the muscles no longer flexed and the heart beat indifferently. The rooms were still dark around her: the front room where Pack's book was spread flat on the carpet beside his coffee mug, a book on snow leopards and survival; their bedroom where his workshirt had been carelessly thrown; the bathroom where Pack taped messages to the mirror—no longer the boyish love notes he'd once left, more like the one there now: . . . *and this our life, when was it truly ours, and when are we truly whatever we are?* from something he had read.

Another chance, she thought, sitting again. She studied the pills lying before her, the tears beginning to burn her eyes. She scraped her hand across the tabletop, scattering the pills across the kitchen, spilling back the chair as she stood and ran out into the darkness of the house, turning on lights, screaming *Goddamn it* at the tears, screaming *No* at the treads of the stairs. *Goddamn it. Goddamn it,* throwing open doors, flipping switches, every one she could lay a hand on, until the whole house was burning and raging with life.

It was dawn again. Dawn of the husbands, Pack thought. He had been quiet all the way back, not letting on to the trucker who'd stopped for him who he was: the man presumed dead. It was still a private affair. The driver played a Willie Nelson tape, mostly ballads, and hummed along in fair harmony, blinking constantly at the road beyond his windshield. Pack hugged his arms inside the sweatshirt the driver had lent him. This was always a nervous and transitional hour, one kind of thought giving way to the next. Pack remembered how much of his life had disappeared working like the driver beside him, only with less sense of destination than this man surely had. He remembered the few times he had left a woman at that hour, the sadness of strange doorways and words that disappear like balloons into an endless sky, the whine of his engine as it carried him away. He thought of Kyle and Rita waking together in their tent, joined by affection and the belief that the only good road leads away from home.

Pack thanked the man and got down from the truck at the edge of town. He walked slapping his arms. The full white moon floated above the unawakened houses, above the familiar rise and fall of the mountains. In the next block somebody's husband had gone out and started a pickup in the semidark. Steam flared from the exhaust. Soon the heater would throw two rings of warm air at the frosted windshield. Pack broke into a run, loping through the empty intersections, cold air slamming into his lungs.

He stopped in the mouth of the short street that deadended at his house. Men on the road talk about coming home religiously, though they are not religious men or even, Pack thought, men who are at peace being there. What they want is to be welcomed each time, their return treated like the consummation of something noble, which is too much to ask. Unnecessary risks, Pack thought, too great and foolish to be rewarded with love. He had somehow thought he was immune.

Panting hard through the gap in his teeth but warm for the first time in many hours, Pack looked up to see the lights blazing from his house, even from the twin attic dormers and the areaway at the basement window. He could never know the fullness of his wife's grief, how it came with as many shades of diminishing light as a summer twilight, just as she would never know why his lonely disposition took him always away from her, or precisely what had happened to change him. Sometimes it is a comfort to believe that one day is like another, that things happen over and over and are the same. But accidents happen, and sometimes a man or a woman is lucky enough to see that all of it, from the first light kiss onward, could have gone another way. Pack ran to the front door of his house, alive, thinking *dawn of homecoming, dawn of immaculate good fortune.*